Edited by
Jan Fook, Susan Hawthorne and Renate Klein

Cat Tales

The Meaning of Cats in Women's Lives

SPINIFEX

Spinifex Press Pty Ltd
504 Queensberry Street
North Melbourne, Vic. 3051
Australia
women@spinifexpress.com.au
http://www.spinifexpress.com.au

First published by Spinifex Press, 2003

Cover and book design by Deb Snibson, The Modern Art Production Group
Made and printed in Australia by McPherson's Printing Group

National Library of Australia
Cataloguing-in-Publication data:

Cat Tales: The meaning of cats in women's lives.

ISBN 1 876756 37 3.

1. Cats - Social aspects. 2. Women and animals. I. Fook, Janis, II. Hawthorne, Susan, 1951- .
   III. Klein, Renate.
   V. Title.

636.80082

For Ned who made us laugh and cry.

Contents

Section One   CATachievers   1

Section Two   CATalogues   31

Acknowledgements

Many women were involved in putting this book together and we gratefully acknowledge their assistance. First, we want to thank Belinda Morris who co-ordinated all aspects of finding contributors, choosing which pieces to include, matching the best photographs of cats and their women with the contributions, and liaising with authors, designer and editors. Belinda's great organisational skills and hard work, as well as her never-ending enthusiasm for animals, made working on this project a joy, without any headaches. Thank you Belinda, for your invaluable support for all of us and for your wonderful dry humour; we know cats are not dogs but we knew you were smitten when we heard you oohing over the gorgeous cat pics we received!

We also thank the other women working at Spinifex Press—Maralann Damiano, Laurel Guymer, Elana Markowitz and Jo O'Brien—who welcomed the idea of a 'cat book' after the successful 'dog book' and contributed their knowledge of cat women to help us find contributors. We also thank them for their ideas on cover, design and publicity. No cat-story-author amongst them this time—we guess they might be waiting for the horses? the birds? the wild animals? to tell their tales.

Designer Deb Snibson proved yet again what creativity in design can produce and with energy and passion created the bold yet elegant look we wanted to achieve. We especially love the cover design which so cleverly embodies Susan Hawthorne's title of the book with the cat's tail smoothly sliding over the page. And, after the daring pink and orange we chose for the dogs, we think that we have captured the perhaps more enigmatic mood of cats and their women with the beautiful green/blue colour scheme. Thank you Deb for yet again patiently accommodating our wishes for exciting and 'different' design and for the warmth you brought to this job which this time also included typesetting: a very successful double act.

We also thank Barbara Burton who copy-edited the book and, like us, had great pleasure in reading about the funny, the naughty and the brave cats—and their women—whose tales appear in this book.

A special thank you must go to Elana and son Jonathan who offered their cat Aladdin for a photo shoot although Aladdin wasn't too impressed with the experience (and we found out that cats can't be tricked with treats in the way dogs can). Susan proved to be the most acceptable cat woman amongst us and photographer Naomi Mc Kercher did a great job capturing our pleasure at seeing another beautiful animal book taking shape whilst wishing that Aladdin was a little more impressed with our purr and miaow imitations.

Finally we want to thank each other for yet another joyful partnership and co-operation that made us laugh a great deal—and, at times, even cry for the cats. Jan, Belinda and Renate happily deferred to Susan's poetry expertise but thank her for allowing us our favourite poem—we leave for the readers to guess which one it is.

And last but, of course, not least, a great thank you to all contributors and their cats, past and present. May the cats in this book join the dogs in *A Girl's Best Friend*—and we're already looking forward to more fun with *HorseDreams* to which we'll be turning soon.

Jan Fook
Susan Hawthorne
Renate Klein

Preface

Jan Fook, Susan Hawthorne and Renate Klein

What do animals mean in the life of humans? This is a question asked increasingly, especially when, in countries like Australia and the United States, two-thirds of households own at least one pet. Studies abound which demonstrate that pets can save lives or at least sanity, and that people can grieve as deeply for a lost pet as for the loss of human companionship. It is intriguing then to hear about some of these experiences, and to try to understand in more depth how our furry friends weave themselves inextricably into our homes, our lives, our very existence.

This special volume, on the meaning of cats in women's lives, is the second in a series on what companion animals mean to women around the globe. When Spinifex Press published *A Girl's Best Friend: The Meaning of Dogs in Women's Lives*, a clamour went up from women and cats for a further volume. We agreed and the experience of compiling this collection has been wonderful. We asked women from as diverse backgrounds as possible to contribute and received pieces from women in many different countries, and of different ages and cultural backgrounds. The contributions reflect this diversity. We have funny, sad and clever pieces. We have pieces which address the political and socially serious side of having cats as pets. We have pieces which reflect the sometime silliness of domestic life with cats. We have poems, short stories, reflections and essays.

What has emerged is a clear picture of the different relationships women have with feline companions because of the distinctive characteristics of cats, both as animals and as individuals. They enrich our lives in different ways simply because they are not humans, they are not dogs, birds, horses or monkeys. Cats mean distinctive things to different women.

What is the nature and meaning of this relationship? Some contributors describe it by distinguishing the characteristics of cats from those of dogs. The saying 'Dogs have masters, cats have staff' was quoted several times. Another idea voiced by many women is that of the cat as 'familiar', alluding to an almost mystical relationship with a creature who is only a visitor to the human world. The naming of cats, and the special task of creating a name that captures the magnificent, regal and independent character of a particular animal, is also a notable thread in many stories. Some women rush to rescue abandoned litters. And cats often return such nurturing, and provide a supportive presence, in times of emotional and social vulnerability.

We have grouped the pieces around some of the main themes that characterised the contributions for us. The section of CATachievers tries to capture cats of character, the ones whose extraordinary quirks and habits have endeared them to us forever. CATalogues contains stories of a series of cats in a lifetime. Sometimes no one cat is more special than another, but through all of them we are able to trace the nuances of our lives and some of our own quirks. CATalysts recognises the cats whose presence in women's lives has wrought remarkable, and sometimes necessary change. Sometimes these cats bring a new way of seeing, or simply offer companionship when that is a woman's premium need. CATastrophes tells the stories of cats whose achievements were not always welcome, but which nonetheless enriched women's lives.

CATacombs include stories of totally memorable cats who have now passed on. And AristoCATS belong to that category of cats who almost defy categorisation. These are the elite, majestic creatures, owned by no one but themselves, but who nevertheless manage to inspire devotion and even a sense of worship.

Yet despite the many different ways in which women and girls experience the company of cats, it is perhaps the common threads which speak the loudest—the recognition that our cats, and perhaps any of our companion animals, provide us with that sense of connectedness with another creature which goes beyond human relationships. On the one hand, they depend on us more completely than any human being. On the other, they belong to a world which we can never fully inhabit. To experience the abundant delights of this relationship we must create a shared space. And what seems to matter most are not the differences between cat or dog lovers, but the recognition that the challenge of creating a shared space, with whatever creature, is what sustains and develops us as human beings.

Cat Tales doesn't just tell us about the relationships of women with cats; it tells us about who we are as human beings. 🐾

Section One CATachievers

Mrs Black: A True Cat Story

Lin Van Hek

It was during the time that our family suffered a series of misfortunes too numerous and dismal to mention and we found ourselves homeless and living out of our car.

As chance would have it, a farmer in our district who had recently built himself a vanilla-coloured brick monstrosity, and was feeling uncharacteristically generous, offered us rent-free a derelict out-building on his property to live in.

This was not only a farming district, it was also coastal and the old house, though it had no doors or windows with glass intact, was very close to the ocean. The tide came up close to its timber walls, a prime reason it had been abandoned as a residence years ago.

We could not drive our car down the rutted and heavily treed track that led to the house. We left our car ten minutes from the house and, loaded up with our belongings, we ran down there, through spotted gums, the air fragrant with ti-tree blossom and the salty ocean.

It was here that we met the cat.

She stood in the doorway large and black all over. She had no idea that she was a cat. She did not move to let us by. She stood her ground. Her shoulders filled the doorway. Our mother cautioned us to take it easy. The cat looked us over. One large, four small, she seemed to calculate. Moments passed, we held our breath, then the cat lost interest and walked regally away into the bush.

The cat did not accept any food from us though in our monthly buying trip to town we bought cat food and offered her milk. She declined the offer.

She slept inside the house always on our beds. Over the next year we were given two other cats but she showed no inclination to befriend or consider herself familiar with them.

She did however like dogs. All our friends had dogs and they always brought them along on visits. She greeted them, sat amongst them, overpowered them. It was obvious they thought her a superior dog, one of their species.

We stopped being curious about what she ate. She never brought home a catch and the old house was free of rats and mice. Since our mother was concentrating on feeding us, she was anxious to get her garden going and pleased that the cat only needed a bowl of fresh water from the tank. At first we called that cat Colette, blinded by her theatrical feline presence. She never did answer to this name and ceased all eye contact when we tried to make it stick.

Finally, we called her Mrs Black. She became famous in the district. They even talked about her in town. Mrs Black sightings were a major topic of conversation. She was the cat belonging to that odd writer woman who lived with her four children in the old house with no electricity, right on the ocean. Mrs Black the cat was quick to answer to this name. She travelled widely by foot and had other homes that she would stay in for days at a time. If she was walking near a homestead and someone called out 'Hey, Mrs Black!' she would stride into the house and stay awhile.

One time, she was missing for a couple of weeks. We missed her badly. When she came back she walked through our house, still with no doors and settled herself in the back bedroom where my mother slept. In the night she had kittens. Eight of them fought for space at her belly and for the first time she accepted the milk we collected each day from our farmer neighbour.

When the kittens were a few days old she started disappearing again, often during the night. In the morning she would be cleaning herself in the sun until every square inch of that black coat shimmered with light. Our mother would whisper as if to a lover, 'What an exquisite beautiful cat you are, Mrs Black.'

The cat would arch her head into the woman and they would both stay awhile, locked together, eyes closed in the morning sun.

One morning at dawn, down the track, now made wider by constant use, came a group of farmers on horseback, a few of their sons on motorbikes at the back.

'We want Mrs Black!'

Our mother recognised a posse; it was a little after dawn they had called her from her bed. 'She's not here,' she told them. 'What's the matter?'

'She's killing our chooks and now she's started on the sheep.'

They all had guns; they came into the house, saw the kittens and waited for Mrs Black's return. My mother made endless cups of tea after starting the outside fire. We did not have enough cups and the men passed the cups between them. We children were excited by the fervour.

'Mrs Black's a killer,' they told us with authority.

The sensitive ones tried to break it to us gently that they were here to shoot her. Mrs Black did not return. The men rode off; they had other chores to get on with they told each other.

After the sun had gone down Mrs Black came home. We children saw her go to our mother's room, stepping lightly over the timber floorboards; we saw our mother remove the tiny bell that she had fixed around Mrs Black's neck.

Next day at dawn the men returned. Mrs Black and the kittens were gone. The men were angry now. They were fed up they said with the cat and us. They shook their fists at our mother then they turned their horses around and went home. Mrs Black did not return.

One day we went to town to buy supplies for the next few months. It was our big trip to town. Our house was very comfortable now. We were doing correspondence lessons from the education department every day. Our mother wrote a story that won the *Age* newspaper short story contest with a prize that bought us new doors for our house. The garden was full of tomatoes and lettuces and herbs that we watered from the tank.

'We made it,' said our mother every now and then in the middle of everything.

We returned to our house from our shopping expedition as happy as we'd ever been. As we came upon our house we got the shock of our lives. Men with a bulldozer were pulling down our house.

'It's not your house,' reminded the farmer who had given us this house rent-free. He stood there and allowed us to load our car with our life. 'You can get a caravan in the caravan park real cheap.'

We piled our belongings onto the roof rack of our car and filled our washing basket with food from the garden before the bulldozer wiped it out.

You'll be pleased to hear that these bad times didn't last, for our mother bought some land in the mountains in the middle of the State Forest. There we lived in a house we built ourselves from river rock. Our garden was filled with fruit trees and sunflowers, asparagus and strawberries and we were richer than anyone has a right to be. We were about seventy-five miles from our old home that was bulldozed but even so everyone in this new place knew our story.

One day, our mother was on her knees in the marjoram freeing it from the grasses that were strangling it; the sun was warming her back.

She felt a slight pressure against her hip and thinking it was one of us children she turned sleepily with a smile. She whispered and her voice was lost in the mountain air, 'Oh, what an exquisite beautiful cat you are, Mrs Black.'

Lin Van Hek is a country woman by birth and inclination. She has had several meaningful relationships with exceptional animals. She has spent ten years travelling with her performing group, Difficult Women (http://www.starnet. com.au/dwomen/) meeting thousands of women with the same inclinations. She is presently working on a sequel to her book, The Ballad of Siddy Church; *working title:* The Difficult Women's Cookbook, *an adventuresome tale of travel and intrigue and women eating three times a day.*

Window Cats

Diane Fahey

Presences behind glass:
their otherness glitters,
draws me up the path to gaze at
their indecipherable dream.

One curves, pure black, along
the saddle of the rocking horse;
the second, a porcelain shape,
tabbily perfect under
the chipped grey nostrils:
both poised, in possession,
and every hair a masterstroke.

Behind slits in topaz
each is an intimate absence
staring me back down the path,
the tabby leaping into
the window frame to watch me away,

then vanishing into that
stillness, that composed power,
on which they ride and they fly
to old Assyria.

Diane Fahey *lives at Barwon Heads,
on the south-east coast of Victoria.
Her seven poetry collections deal with
nature, myths and fairy tales, and
autobiography. Her last book,* The
Sixth Swan, *is based on Grimm's fairy
tales. She is currently writing a book of
poetry about Barwon Heads.*

Climbing Roofs

Lorraine Williams

Midnight. A friend had dropped me off at the end of the street when a flash of white caught my eye on the roof of number one.

A small chocolate-smudged face with flapping bat-like ears leaned over the guttering and screeched, *'Yowwwww-OW-OWWWWW!'*

The gremlins had landed!

It wasn't a gremlin. It was StarGirl, my young Siamese cat. 'Goodness, what are you doing up there?' I hissed. 'How'd you get on the roof of that house?'

She shrugged. *'Mee-yoww? It was here, so I climbed it. Did they third-degree Hillary when he conquered Everest? No, that man got a medal... and all you want to do is tell me off.'*

'I suppose I could leave you up there till morning,' I said.

My cat bristled. *'Morning? Forget morning.'* StarGirl, being StarGirl wanted to be got down NOW!

I'd knock on the door of number one, I decided, tell the kind widow-woman who lived there about StarGirl being on her roof, ask to borrow a ladder, and get bat-ears down.

No. Three things were wrong with that scenario. One, no kind widow-woman lived in the house. It was an old crab who hated cats and laid out cat deterrent in her garden. Two, I knew that the crab didn't possess a ladder... and Three, the house was in total darkness; the crab had been in the Land of Nod for hours and wouldn't take kindly to being woken just for the sake of a cat, even if that cat was truly the greatest one in the entire world.

I would have to conduct a secret operation. I got my own ladder from the garage. Dropping the catch on the crab's front gate, there was a loud TWA-A-A-A-NG!! as it slammed back against the wall of the house. I stood petrified for a good five minutes. No reaction from inside number one.

StarGirl's howling was loud as I progressed closer, ladder under arm, banging the ladder first against a camellia tree, and then so hard against a terracotta mermaid I almost took its head off. I anchored the ladder into some geraniums. Tentatively I placed a foot on the bottom rung and discovered how hopeless it was to climb in peepy-toe high-heels. I cast them aside. The rungs were cold on my panty-hosed feet.

Don't look down, I told myself, you are an intrepid mountaineer. You can do this. I climbed unsteadily upwards. The last rung was the worst. I towered above the top of the ladder, with just my knees anchored behind a small aluminium safety barrier. 'Here StarGirl-StarGirl-StarGirl ...'

I stretched out my arms for the baby to hop into them. What a time for a cat to suddenly become shy.

'Naw, you'll only drop me.' She backed away.

'Come here, StarGirl!' I snapped.

She shook her head... and started to clean herself, serenely, in an unmentionable place.

'If you come home with me,' I said cunningly, 'I promise to buy you a box of those completely unhealthy crunchies that the vet said were no good for your urinary system but you totally adore ever since you got through the catflap of Leo-from-next-door and stole his.'

'*Yow*?' StarGirl sauntered over. '*Welllll, Alriiiiight, I guess I do need a lift down.*'

Cat under one arm, ladder under the other—I forgot my peepy-toe high-heels in the rush to get away and had to sneak back later and retrieve them from the geraniums—I sloped up my street as naturally as I could manage it. Well, you never knew who might be watching.

A week or two later I saw StarGirl again on the roof of number one. '*Yoo-hoo, Mum, here I am. Don't bother with the ladder. I've always known the way down.*'

She leapt from roof, to fence, to grass, without a backward look... and sauntered up to me. '*How's it doin', mate? Okay?*'

But all had not been for naught. My experience with ladders came in handy when the crab—yes, her from number one—rushed down the street hysterically yelling there was a cat, a stray, on her roof. Wasn't there anybody—'For God's sake, Anybody?' the woman shouted, 'who can get this animal down?' I raised a hand nobly. 'I volunteer,' I said.

It was a doddle, a breeze. Nobody realised I was a ladder-climbing professional, especially when it came to this particular house. Hoorays, hosannas, and verbal bouquets were tossed at my feet.

It turned out the cat had been trapped on the roof for three nights, during torrential rain, and without any food. The crab—who in the end turned out to be a bit of a pussycat herself—gave me a big hug and a pot of homemade stew that I shared with StarGirl. I figured it was only right to give my cat some. Without bat-ears, I wouldn't have become a hero. The way I see it, it's always a good idea to practise at it—being a hero, that is—before you're actually asked to take on the job.

*In her teens, **Lorraine Williams** never thought twice about cats. In her twenties, she found herself oohing and ahhing over cat calendars. By the time she turned thirty, Lorraine was burrowing under parked cars to pat a cat or going a block out of her way to cuddle one in a stranger's driveway. In her early forties, she thought deeply about the responsibilities of living with a feline and, by the time Lorraine hit fifty, StarGirl the Siamese had turned the Williams residence into a two female household. StarGirl figures it's good to have a full-time hand-maiden, especially now that Lorraine has taken early retirement from her job as a staff training officer.* 🐾

Burmese Days

Suzanne Bellamy

I wonder if the Great Cat Mothers of antiquity realised the frisson their ancestral line would embody in their great journey through the world of the humans? Yes, it meant they could implant our brains with brilliant inventions like fire and doonas and Italian sofas. They could be great teachers of meditation, indifference, detachment and gourmet fish in a tin. They perfected early miniaturisation so as to fit into any armpit of their choice, and experienced early weightlessness rising and falling on the breath of a human chest. On the whole, they avoided being eaten, farmed, fenced in, trained, used in battle.

This, of course, is propaganda. Not all cats gave consent, were taken in by the seductions of advertising and easy adoration, not all cats want aesthetic apolitical amnesic lives. Some cats have always been revolutionary, anarchic, street-loving, dangerous, comic and subversive. These tend to be the cats I have attracted and, in all the years of worship and devotion they have accepted from me with reluctance, they have also been a generous challenge, literally in my face on the core issues of existential being.

Myths of origin were settled early, as we watched the first Russian satellite some time in the late 1950s. I got to sit up on my brother's FJ Holden car-hood in the dark night with Dad, looking into space, allowed to stay up to see this wonder. All our cats from then were called Sputnik, with added numbers 1,2,3,4. Always black cats, living under the house or in the chook-feed shed, never allowed inside by my mother, and endless kittens who created the first dramas of life and death.

Long lines of cats fill my nostrils, heart and memory cells. Terrible deaths on the road, or from ticks, from dogs, from mysterious vanishings. They were in my pack, in my arms, under my chin, part of the life. Later I lived in Glebe and Annandale for many years, as a student, academic and artist, always with cats. Back lanes, cat piss smells, raided garbage, short lives out there on the street, co-existing with the well-fed contemplatives in the windows of terrace houses as you walked down Glebe Point Road.

I have too many cat stories, all sharp edged. Here's one draft, in my mini cat series.

Burmese Days, Annandale in the early 1980s, Paris End, Left Bank.

We lived in Alfred Street, Annandale, in two adjoining houses, in a lesbian relationship of structural independence more than flawless autonomy. Four cats inhabited this geography with more libertine energy than we ever did. Two houses can be a pain in the arse. Two beloved cats were killed on the street, and buried under the *Eucalyptus cinereria* in the tiny backyard. But my Burmese girl walked through it all. Cinnamon, named for her colour statement and the trancy body smell of riches from the Orient, still holds the record for my longest relationship: seventeen years. She arrived as a gift a year after I moved from Glebe to Alfred Street in 1978, where we fused in lovers goo. Alfred Street had a certain creative lesbian ambience even then, and everyone had cats. In the back lanes were many more cats, lacking passports and affiliation, outnumbering both the humans and the cat insiders. Lesbian rock bands, writers, broadcasters, witches and artists filled up the little cottages, as edgy then as the cats in some ways.

In one lived the marvellous Hephaista and the women from the Stray Dags, a lesbian rock band. Right next door to me though was definitely not Lesbian Nation. Here was Audrey, a very sweet neighbour really but with a horrible occasional boyfriend called Wayne (married to a woman a street away, shock horror) who had a truck he always parked outside my house and started up at 5 a.m, some mornings. It was outrageous, even for us. Audrey had been a nurse I think but then decided to work from home, in her illegal basement garage. I could see all this from my big back kitchen window. In no time, she had several of her women friends working there in what I was convinced was a kind of Small Arms Factory. That's what I called it anyway, and nothing was the same after Audrey got into munitions.

Cinnamon was a skitty cat, and there were too many dogs in this little street. All I can say is that she must have been given a terrible fright by the dog that came to Audrey's that day. Anyway she ended up on the absolute very top of the wooden telegraph pole outside Audrey's, no kidding. I rang the fire-brigade and they said 'lady you've seen too much TV' and laughed at the idea they would come and save my cat. So many neighbours came out to help, cups of tea, useless optimistic ideas, all gazing at the livewires and the pole.

There was Hephaista, who I met for the first time that day. She said she was a witch and so I was very hopeful. Of course, the whole Small Arms Factory poured out onto the street too, and attempts with poles and other implements were made as hours passed. By then I was in post, post-telegraph trauma. The horrible boyfriend even turned up with the truck, and finally Audrey (a born military leader it emerged) got everyone to bring out tables of many sizes, then we piled them up from large to small until they reached somewhere near the top of the pole, with a ladder hauled up over the tables.

It was like an Oriental painting. Audrey sent the awful boyfriend up on the perilous table-and-ladder climb and finally he managed to dislodge Cinnamon enough to grab her, as the tables threatened to topple. This you realise was in the days before a women's circus. Finally she was saved. I vomited at last. The boyfriend was covered in blood. Burmese show no gratitude you know.

●●●●●

Life with cats is so complex. We finally moved from that house in 1983 and went to live in the country. What a relief. It was best for everyone. But Cinnamon was a brilliant sleek killer, and in the country she found endless baby rabbits to bring in, through the cat-and-dog door onto the carpets, to eat at leisure. My great commitment to her and the other animals sat in stark contrast with the bush, other ferals, wildlife and another kind of real world.

I worked through some kind of compromise until she finally retired from hunting, and her last years were less dramatic. She had to deal with Thelma our new dog and many other problems, but she was always number one under the doona. Now she is buried here at Mongarlowe, the last cats and Thelma too.

I miss having cats; I still see them occasionally in the bush. It doesn't work, but then there are the foxes and rabbits and pigs and wild goats too. The great human caravan has spread so many troubles, but in the end what I know from my cats is the need to be in it fully, to make the space in the heart for the contradictions of attachment. I have made friends with a little lizard who lives in front of my kiln and comes into the bathroom, under the door, sometimes for water. She smiles, she lets you know when she is around with a tail swish. One day she drank out of the end of the dribbling hose as I held it out to her. Cinnamon would have eaten her; what can I say? Life moves on.

Suzanne Bellamy is an Australian artist and writer based in southern NSW. She exhibits sculpture and printmaking internationally, lives in a rural studio on land with native animals, is writing a novel saga about the early women's movement in Australia, is a Virginia Woolf scholar, and is trying to explore a crossover art/thought form called the visual essay. 🐾

The Mother Cats

Melinda Tankard Reist

One of the biggest thrills of my childhood growing up on a fruit property in country Victoria was discovering the newest litter of kittens.

Our community of cats—twenty-six at its peak—had at its core three we called The Mother Cats: Tabitha, better known as Tabsy, a tabby grey; the Black-and-White Mother Cat, our most beautiful cat, and a motley coat-of-many colours cat called Mizzy. They were always having kittens. We felt so lucky!

An excited cry would erupt from one of us four kids when we found the latest batch—under the house, in the shed, under shrubs and orange trees, in an underground cement cavity. Tabsy preferred the blue-and-white antique pram full of mum's old nightdresses and petticoats.

We'd rustle up old eiderdowns and whatever else we thought they needed for their comfort, then divide the kittens between us. I always picked the runt. They would then be named and lovingly watched as they fed from their mother—well, actually, any mother who happened to lie down beside them. The mothers shared the feeding and rearing of the kittens. Sometimes I'd re-arrange them on the nipples to make sure the milk was being fairly distributed and my littlest one wasn't missing out.

My mother would allow us to give the mother cats extra bowls of milk when they were feeding kittens. Mum would also throw them liver from the back door and Dad would toss them the heads and guts from fish he'd been filleting in the backyard.

The cats had it pretty tough, surviving on grasshoppers, mice, scraps and the half-can of dog food they shared. (I'd sometimes sneak them an extra half-can of Tucker Box if I thought I could get away with it). They were scrawny, mangy and flea-ridden (we'd rest them on our knees, sprawled on their backs as we doused them in a cloud of flea power and plucked the fleas from them). But, in the little extras my parents gave the mother cats, I understood that mothers were to be looked after and cared for.

I have an enduring memory of the bravery and devotion of the mother cats. Black-and-White Mother Cat had given birth during the night under an orange tree, just before the overhead water sprinklers were turned on. In the morning we found her, frozen stiff on all fours, sheltering the kittens with her body. The newborns were dry. We moved them, towelled off their mother and gradually she warmed up. I have never forgotten that single act of pure self-sacrifice.

It was well known that we had lots of cats. And it must have been known that we would care for them or try to find homes for them because there would often be a hessian bag or a box full of tiny mewling kittens to greet us at the end of the driveway on our way to school. Such a weight of responsibility. I had to keep them alive! It was up to me! I'd take the bag to school and try to cajole friends into taking a kitten. I'd then take home the rest and begin the regular round of feeding with eye-droppers with cow's milk. I often had kittens sleeping by my bed in a shoebox, and got up in the night to feed them. I'd fall back to sleep with my hand in the box to comfort them… and me.

But they didn't always survive. 'Min alright?' I'd hear Dad ask my mother, when he'd come inside after having shot a sick kitten. His question made me feel a bit better.

I was often frightened at night by stray male cats howling eerily around the orange trees outside my bedroom window. The terrible sound of them fighting. I'd fear for the mothers and their kittens and hiss at these shadowy ghosts through the window to try to scare them off. Sometimes, if I felt very brave, I'd go outside in the dark and throw oranges at them.

I settled a black-and-white runt kitten with tiny white whiskers and blue eyes in a doll's cradle in the shed. The next morning I found it suffocated between the slats of the cradle. I convinced myself it had died because it was very sick. I couldn't bear to think I'd killed it, that I'd failed in my duty to care for that which was entrusted to me.

But most recollections are happy.

In summer I would climb up a tree and onto the shed roof. My sister would put a bunch of kittens in a tin (also containing books and snacks) tied with rope and I'd lift them up to join us. We'd laze away entire afternoons lying on a mattress on the roof with the kittens.

When seriously ill in bed for months with a mysterious blood disease which turned me into a waif with black growths on my lips and hair falling out, I'd sometimes sneak kittens in to my room. There'd be two or three frolicking in the bed or asleep and purring under my blanket.

I recovered.

Melinda Tankard Reist *is a Canberra writer and author of*
Giving Sorrow Words: Women's Stories of Grief after Abortion
(Duffy and Snellgrove, 2000). She has four children but,
sadly, no kittens for them to play with.

Castaway

June Kant

He came in after midnight. Like all good mothers I'd been keeping an ear out for him, sleeping lightly, until I knew he was back aboard. We had arrived late in a small Greek harbour and Panzudo, our Spanish crew, had abandoned ship to explore his latest landfall. The first I knew of his return was a sudden weight beside me on the bunk and the cool touch of his nose against my face. Without opening my eyes I acknowledged his greeting and encountered at stroke's end what felt like a muddy tail. In my mind I envisaged the dirty blanket, imagined the hand washing, and in annoyance pushed Panzudo to the floor. Moments later I heard him scrabble into an open locker in the forepeak. He seemed unsettled but he was home and safe—that was all that mattered.

Morning sun funnelled its way through the porthole and I surfaced slowly, remembering with dismay the mud. Strangely, there was none but the eiderdown was newly patterned with white splotches. White? My puzzled gaze followed a trail of white footprints across the floor to the forepeak. Fully awake now, I left the bed to look for Panzudo. He wasn't in the locker where he had gone when banished but the toolbags there were encrusted with the same white substance. I moved aft to the main cabin and observed white paw-prints across the table, his usual route when entering via a porthole. I wondered at the mahogany bulkhead newly sprigged in a white pattern and flicks of white decorating the overhead beams. A clunk diverted my attention—there was Panzudo sitting on the top step of the companionway, his bulk silhouetted in the hatch.

'Hello, Fat One. What on earth did you get up to last night?'

He sprang from the ladder, and as he crash-landed at its foot my question was answered. In horrified fascination I moved closer to examine him.

Panzudo was in a cast from his undercarriage downwards. He had waded through a builder's plaster-pit and the gypsum had now set. The luxuriant fur of his belly had formed into solid white udders. His granola-textured shanks atrophied into skeletal legs. His paws were clubbed. His tabby back and head were untouched but his tail, slickly encased, dragged low. His usual arrogance, however, would admit to no image-impairment—he hadn't come for pity. It was breakfast he wanted.

My first thought was to wash him. I prayed, without adequate faith, that the plaster would dissolve. Hastily I dropped a bucket over the side and hauled it brimming to the deck. Ignoring the usual quayside observers, I grabbed my unsuspecting victim and dunked him. His affronted reaction was to struggle and bite his way out of my grip and the bucket—over the side and into the harbour. My exasperation turned to horror with the realisation that a cat cast in plaster would sink which sent me scrambling for the scoop net. Adding insult to injury, the bystanders cheered his undignified retrieval. With a mortified hiss and yowl he clomped with bedraggled hauteur below decks. My comfort was churlishly rebuffed. There was no question of towel-drying the angered Panzudo. Rage activated his solid tail—clonk, bang, clonk—it slammed the table on which he sat and I immediately realised the cause of the spatters on the bulkhead and beams—the same tail-swishing exasperation had flicked wet plaster last night. If only I had helped him then. Now the most I could do was leave him in peace—and feed him, for nothing could impair the appetite of Panzudo.

The captain, on sight of the new-model of ship's cat, broke into unfeeling laughter. Clonk, bang, clonk, bang—Panzudo's angry tail doubled the hilarity. His claws were encased and out of action, but his teeth were unencumbered. The laughter stopped. Alas, his handicap hindered an escape and yet again his dignity was forced to suffer.

My heart bled for him. His fate and his body were sealed for the foreseeable future—until he could be free of his cast he was immobilised and boat-bound, anathema to a roustabout cat in a new harbour. Out of sympathy we set sail.

Panzudo's humour was poor during his voyage of recuperation—a cat afloat without sea legs is only marginally less discontented than a cat with suspended

shore leave. With ferocity he refused all attempts at assistance but each time he slept I made lightning attacks with scissors to cut away sections of fur. While every clump less helped recovery of movement, it did nothing to improve his appearance nor his irascibility. While I snipped during his sleep, his every waking hour was spent plucking with his teeth. His priority was to free his paws and persistently, hour after hour, he gnawed and teased to remove the wedges from between his toes until his pads were raw. He limped, but regained his sure-footedness. Next he attended to his tail, removing its excess baggage and thus restoring his balance. The boat was strewn with crisp tufts of fur and his appearance became daily more comical but compassion and caution precluded laughter in his presence.

By the time we made landfall the tabby spots on his rotund belly had gone the way of their soft ginger fur lining, removed fastidiously until no trace of the cruel crust remained. It was Christmas Eve and he closely resembled an oven-ready, plucked and stuffed turkey.

Uncharacteristically, Panzudo did not rush headlong into his next shore leave. Perhaps, despite his bold disposition, he realised that there are indeed, more ways than one to kill a cat. Getting plastered in a foreign port is not a recommended way to go.

June Kant's *many years abroad on a sailing yacht have provided the rich material and experiences on which she now draws for her fiction. Since her return to Brisbane in 2000, June has won more than half-a-dozen awards for her short stories (many of which have also been aired nationally on radio) and has had various of her non-fiction articles published by The Society of Editors, Qld. Her current work-in-progress is a radio play which she hopes will be aired early next year.* 🐾

Daffodil Goes to the Gym

Annabel Fagan

'**Tell me a story,**' my kid said, 'eh Mum.'

'Whaddabout?' I said, mumbled really. A reluctant mumble. I was deep in a Xena Warrior Princess comic.

'About Spiderman swinging from a chimney and catching robbers.'

'No.'

'About the races.'

'Races?'

'Or PE. I like PE at school.'

'Oh, all right, PE then.'

'Or Daffodil catching the bus to the mall to buy me a present.'

'We've done that one, shut-up now and listen.'

•••••

'Daffodil wanted muscles. "How can I get muscles," she asked you.'

'She should've asked you, Mum, you've got *big* ones.'

'Well, she's your cat. In any case, you told her to go to the gym. "How," said Daffodil, "it's too far." "Hitch-hike," you said, "go on don't be a scaredy cat." Daffodil said "up you" with her tail and sat on the step in the sun to think. I'll internalise the male human space and take it over, turn it into feline, thereby making it pure, she thought.'

'What?' said my kid.

'Shush,' I said. 'She just thinks cats shouldn't be discriminated against, especially female cats with beautiful, yellow eyes.'

'Oh.'

'So she decides and stalks up the drive. Stump, stump, she walks. Frankly I think she has plenty of muscle already.'

'So do I,' my kid said. 'She's tough Daffodil, Queen of the Street.'

'"Well I don't," said Daff, "so mind your own business." She stuck out her grey paw and someone stopped straight away.'

'Yey!' my kid shouted.

'"Where to?" asked the driver. "To the gym, to the gym, to the gym, gym, gym," purred Daff. So off they went.'

'What sort of car,' my kid asked.

'A Rolls Royce, of course. Caused quite a stir when she leapt out. "Make way!" the driver shouted.'

'Yes,' my kid sang, 'make way for Daffodil, Queen of New Zealand. Did she have to pay? You have to pay to get in.'

'Of course not. She just walked in, tail high, they didn't ask. And you should have seen her on the trapeze and high-wire, talk about pure space and past the post anything.'

'Ye-e-e-y!'

'She did it all, lifted weights, jogged, wow—she was better than anyone else. And so strong. "Look at me," she yelled, flying through the air. "Look at me," lifting weights bigger than her. And everyone did. "Is this a cat gym," someone asked. "It is," said Daff, " but you can use it now because I'm going home for my dinner. Where's that Rolls?"'

'Did she have chicken and chips?'

'Yes, and icecream with chocolate sauce.'

'Can we have that?'

'All right, but you've got to watch TV for a while.'

'Now?'

'Now.'

'OK,' my kid said, 'come on Daff.'

Annabel Fagan *is a fourth generation Wellingtonian New Zealander of Irish and English descent. She is lesbian/feminist mum to a beloved son Joshi, aged thirty. Her environment while growing up was very catley and she can't imagine life without a feline companion to dribble and purr over her. She lives a hedonistic life in Paekakariki near Wellington and enjoys talking, walking, reading, writing and eating—especially. She also adores wine.* 🐾

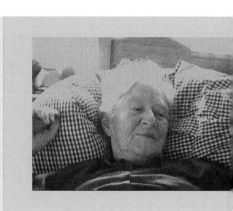

Two and Two
Helen Litchfield

All my life I've had cats, of one sort or another. Most of them were garden-variety moggies. Nothing outstanding about them. But one was really special.

I was thirteen and we lived in the Northern Territory of Australia. At that time, in addition to the usual clutter of cats, we also had a young blue heeler cattle dog. The cats, as they do, had litters of kittens every so often but the dog, due to the absence of a potential father, remained without puppies. Obviously she felt this was unfair and proceeded to do something about it.

In the garden shed there were several old kerosene cases, roughly lined with straw. This is where the cats and the dog usually slept. One night, one of the cats had four kittens and, when my mother found them in the morning, they were all cosily tucked up in the cat's box. But later that day, the cat had two kittens, and the dog, in the adjoining box, also had two.

Mother scolded the dog and returned the two kittens to their cat-mum so they would get a feed. A couple of hours later, when she checked, it was two and two again. This time, when she went to pick up the kittens, the dog showed her teeth. Mother left the kittens where they were.

In spite of her 'virginal' state, the kittens' suckling must have brought on milk, and the dog reared her two stolen children quite satisfactorily. The only difference lay in the fact that the cat licked *with* the fur so that her two were always sleek and trim, whereas the dog licked *against* the fur, and her pair looked as if they had been hauled through a hedge backwards.

As they grew older, the kittens wandered off, as young animals do, and one day we noticed the mother cat worrying about, meowing her head off. One of her kittens was missing. Kittens often disappeared, mainly due to snakes, so we thought that this must have been the little one's fate.

Then we saw the cat march purposefully up to the dog who was snoozing in her box. For a minute or two, the mothers stood nose to nose and even the dumbest human being could see that they were holding a serious conference. Then the dog got up and the two animals disappeared.

A while later, mother called, 'Hey, come and have a look at this!' A small procession was coming down the track. In front was the dog, head up and tail waving and looking smug as only a dog can look. Next came the missing kitten, very meek and subdued. Finally came mother cat, tail high and absolutely oozing satisfaction, bringing up the rear.

Cat-mum took the saved kitten into her box and gave her a good licking down. The dog went back to her box and rolled up to sleep.

Don't anyone ever tell me that animals don't talk!

Helen Litchfield is eighty-six years old and was brought up in the Northern Territory where she was the only white child within five hundred miles. She was Australia's first female aircraft engineer and has worked in England and South Africa, travelled widely in Australia, and now lives on an orchard in outback Queensland.

Pele Aloha
Cathie Dunsford

Pele Aloha was named after the Hawai'ian Godddess of the Volcano: Pele. She was pitch-black like the lava rocks and she had the fiery, cheeky energy of her namesake, a woman who turned her brother into a shark. Pele stole my heart as a kitten and was weaned from her mother too early and left with me to nurture her. I was living in hut in the bush at Tawharanui, had no hot running water and got milk for her from a nearby farmer. I had to kneel down and teach her how to lick, turning my tongue backwards as cats do. She thought it was a riot and thus began her delight in eccentricities.

Her first exploit was predictable enough: she climbed a ti palm and I had to climb up and rescue her. But she soon learned new tricks. I had a rope tied between two ti palms for my washing. One palm was higher than the other. She'd climb the palm, jump into the peg container and use it as her own private cable car to the trees below.

Being a cheeky cat, she was hard work but tremendous fun. Since I was living alone among the Tawharanui tree ferns, she would challenge and test my patience constantly. Through this, I learned unconditional loving. I'd chosen to live on my own while working on my first novel and Pele was the perfect companion. She saw me through three more novels and four anthologies before she decided to exit stage left and return to her home in Hawai'iki, to be with her fiery Pele. She died of leukemia at the time I had lymphatic leukemia. Totally unrelated. But it taught me to look after myself much better. I was grief-stricken for months, but I learned from her lessons.

Perhaps Pele's most famous act was to witness and sign the contract for an anthology commissioned by a publishing company. At the time the contract arrived, nobody was in the bay and I could not find anyone to witness it. My car was dead and the beach houses deserted for the season. So I took Pele's paw and together we scrawled her name on the document. I figured I'd be safe as I had a great relationship with that publisher and nothing would go wrong. Months later, there were disputes with their marketing department and I wondered what would happen if Pele ever had to appear in court in my defence.

Pele was best mates with my folks' crazy chihuahua, Basil. One night after we'd had a meal together, they ganged up and we returned from a walk to find them gorging on the last of our chicken casserole. I knew Pele had taught Basil how to get onto the table. Another time, they conspired to get the cat biscuits from the pantry by Pele jumping up and knocking them down and Basil ripping the package open on the floor. Together, they played and feasted well.

Of course, Pele was a classic cat too: her favourite place to sleep was always the manuscript I was working on at the time and she would have to be coaxed away by very devious means, usually food bribes. She also adored sleeping in my mandolin case. Pele would follow me everywhere and loved our daily walks to the beach. She'd play with the piwakawaka (fantails) jumping between them and the tree ferns as we walked the path to the beach and when we got there she would dive onto the branch of the pohutukawa hanging out over the sand. She'd always get a shock when the tide was in and water lay beneath the tree, then wail to the wind until I returned from collecting cockles, pipis and oysters when the tide was out. You could never win!

When she decided to return to Hawai'iki (where all souls go after death), I carved her name and placed her photo onto a piece of rimu from which I'd built our house. It remains at Mohala today, reminding me of her exploits and those of her fiery namesake, Pele. *I still mourn for my totara sapling, so suddenly cut off: Ka whati ra ia taku mahuri totara*. But I laugh and celebrate her life also.

***Cath Dunsford** adores cats and kai moana (seafood) and lives with her partner Karin, sharing time between Orkney Island, Germany and Aotearoa. She is director of Dunsford Publishing Consultants which has brought 158 new writers into print. She is author of the Cowrie novel series and has fifteen books in print and/or translation globally.* dunsford.publishing@xtra.co.nz.

Tiki: The Tale of a Truly Amazing Cat

Caroline Taylor

Pussy cat, Pussy cat, I love you, yes I do.

Since I was a small child, so many cats have come into my life. An early childhood in poverty and long term abuse with frequent moves around the county, I was a child grateful for her animal companions—those classed by humans as 'pets' and those I discovered within the environment of every place I lived.

Cats fascinated me. Their mystical eyes, sleek and silent movements, their independence and that rhythmic and magical purring from deep within. Try as I did, I never could find the source of that purring but I felt sure it was a display meant for my ears only—to soothe me, encourage me and make me believe that I was special...

My earliest memory of our cats is of Tiki, a black-and-white cat who shared my bed, my secret hiding places and various titbits of food sneaked to her under the table. We moved so often but Tiki, like my dog Kimmy, was the one familiar and trusted part of my life. When I was in grade four we moved house again, this time from the country to the city, entailing a distance of more than a hundred kilometres. Tiki arrived safely at the new place but a short time later she disappeared. She had probably been run over said the adults, or had run away somewhere. Months and months passed. My reconnaissance missions around the huge and run-down house

block had failed to find Tiki. We moved so often I thought, what if we move again and *Tiki* is never again to be seen?

Our neighbour at our former country residence had our address to forward mail. My mother was shocked to receive a letter to say that the neighbour had seen Tiki hanging around our old house. The new occupants wondered about this 'stray' cat that was very thin and would not allow herself to be caught. She simply hung around the house. The neighbour had tried to coax Tiki into her home to no avail. She was sighted over a period of about ten days—then nothing. The news seemed incredible. Dear Tiki had travelled more than a hundred kilometres to our former house. My mind could hardly conceive of how Tiki found her way. She had no road map to guide her. She had to travel through a big city that she had never before known. Months passed and in my familiar private counsel with myself, as only hurting children really understand, I tried to make sense of this epic journey by Tiki and wondered what might be happening to her.

Returning home from school one day, as I walked up the driveway I suddenly heard a strange little noise—hardly discernible and hardly recognisable as to the type of animal making the sound. Suddenly, out from a bush walked Tiki!! I could barely believe my eyes and rushed to pick her up—she was so thin I was scared I would break her if I hugged her. Her paws were badly cut and swollen, her fur dull and patchy. My brothers refused to believe it was Tiki because of her appearance—but I knew. I knew it was my beloved Tiki, home from her epic journey. The adults said she must have had a litter of kittens along the way. How did they know I thought, and where were her kittens? What terrible obstacles and ordeals had Tiki overcome in her amazing trek. Slowly she grew strong again and my awe of Tiki grew. I would sit and look into her iridescent green eyes, mesmerised by the light that hit them and made them appear sparkling—like when the sun shines on water. I was certain that only I had the ability to see the crystal type reflections from her eyes. I recall thinking that I had the ability to see right into her very soul (of course animals have a soul!) and therefore knew her more intimately than did others. Soon we moved again. Tiki came. Again she disappeared and a child's heart held hope for her return. She was never to be seen.

S. Caroline Taylor is a passionate animal lover who lives with her partner and a menagerie of animals on their rural property. Caroline is deeply committed to animal welfare, human rights and children's welfare and is currently a post-doctoral fellow.

Hecate the Horrible: The Thirteenth Cat

Beryl Fletcher

I should have known better than to choose this cat. She was thin, starving, post-partum and howling like a banshee. Her kittens were dead and here she was, skin and bone, looking for safety, looking for a home. The other cats at the shelter were mature family cats with fat bodies and sleek fur, smug in their knowledge of suburban gardens and kitty feeders that provided processed food with the mere sweep of a paw. But they bored me. I wanted a cat with spirit, a feline philosopher. Clearly, this stray cat had all her wits about her. She was a survivor, an ex-pet, a mother thrown out on the street with her kittens to fend for herself. Every fibre of her fur quivered with need. I could almost hear her plead, take me, take me. So I did.

Twelve female cats had shared my life until the arrival of this green-eyed hungry bundle of bones. Many of them met violent deaths: snakes, rabbit traps, cars, dogs. Some lived six months, others fourteen years. The twelfth cat was called Psyche, the name given by the ancient Greeks to the soul, spirit or mind. If we define mind as intelligence, then Psyche had the wrong name. She was a beautiful tabby, a real glamour-puss, but a slow learner. It took me ten days to train her to use a cat door. She never learned to open the flyscreen leading out onto the patio. She got old and deaf and was killed by a car at our front gate.

A few months after Psyche's death, Hecate arrived. I realised at once that she was light years ahead of her predecessor when it came to intelligence. Hecate learned the complicated set of cat ladders and the cat flap in a flash. She followed me everywhere, howling and crying. Friends came to view the new pet. Some thought her strange. She behaved more like a dog than a cat. If visitors removed their footwear at the door, Hecate vigorously licked their feet then sat on their shoes. Some of my more unkind friends labelled her a foot-fetishist. Then there was her appearance. After living on the streets, she weighed only one kilogram. She has a long body, and looked more like a thin furry tail than a living cat.

I fed her five times a day to stop her begging for food. But this did not satisfy her. One day, I came home after shopping to find the fridge door open. Hecate had taken out the tin of Jellymeat, removed the plastic cover, and eaten every scrap of the food. The empty tin lay on the kitchen floor. I closed the fridge, blaming myself for leaving it open. That night, I got up to get a drink of water, and the fridge was open again. Another empty tin on the floor. The next day, I sat quietly on the kitchen sofa for two hours waiting for the culprit to appear. Hecate walked to the fridge, inserted a set of claws into the rubber at the side, sprang back with all her strength, and the door opened effortlessly. I placed a heavy iron soup pot against the fridge. She looked at it, looked at me, and sauntered off. Problem solved, except for the fact that I had to move the damned pot every time I wanted to open the fridge.

That night, I was awakened by a strange noise. Scritch! Scritch! I sneaked into the kitchen. Hecate had worked out how to move the iron pot. She had jammed herself between the pot and the fridge and was pushing the pot with her head. It was hard work, the pot weighed more than she did, but she had almost moved it away from the rubber seal around the fridge door.

By this time I was beginning to realise that Hecate was like no other cat I had ever owned. Amongst other things, she is an accomplished hunter, specialising in large and rather angry rats with huge teeth that do not appreciate being lugged up a cat ladder into the second storey of a house in the middle of the night. Her problem-solving skills include working out how to come backwards through a locked cat flap and how to break into the expensive and allegedly cat-proof new fridge that we had to buy when she ruined the thermostat on the old one by constantly leaving the door open.

I sometimes wonder if I had named her Cuddles or Puddy instead of Hecate she might have turned out differently. Hecate was an ancient Greek deity who embodied the original female trinity of virgin, mother and crone. In the middle ages, she became associated with midwives and witches and was demonised by the Catholic Church.

Now my Hecate is five years old, still a horrible animal, not at all grateful for being rescued from the street. She rules her territory with an iron claw, she does exactly what she likes, and that is why I love her so.

New Zealand feminist writer **Beryl Fletcher** *has published four novels including:* The Word Burners *and* The Bloodwood Clan *and a volume of memoir,* The House at Karamu. *She has been the recipient of prizes and awards, including a Commonwealth Writers Prize. Her books have been translated into German and Korean.*

Section Two CATalogues

Thelma's Cats

Thelma Solomon

I'm not really mad about cats... but I have four of them!

Matilda, a black-and-white long-haired cat, is queen of the household. When we first met, she was the school-office kitten who thumped on typewriters and had a tray in the principal's office, to the annoyance of the cleaner. Matilda purred her way into everybody's hearts but not their homes.

After a week the principal said, 'What now? The Cat Protection Society?' 'No, of course not!' So Matilda came to my house, about twelve years ago. She sleeps on top of the mantlepiece which is the reason there are hardly any ornaments there—they've gradually been removed. Matilda herself is now one of the main mantlepiece ornaments.

On the other side of the mantlepiece is Titch, the boy. There was a time when three cats used to come onto the front veranda because they'd heard there was a kind lady who wouldn't let a homeless cat go hungry. Is that how it happens? Two of the brave boys used to come to the front and smooth around my legs, look me in the eyes, meow and wait for breakfast. But Titch used to hide in the bushes and only when I left would he creep to the plate to eat his.

I found homes for the two brave boys and then had to take the pathetic little Titch into the house where I still continued to look for a home for him. But most lesbians decided Titch needed a psychiatrist and wouldn't take him on because he ran and hid. So they didn't see his beautiful black face with his curly white whiskers and his dainty white feet. Titch is a licorice tabby. His fur is black with white patches and grey underneath and feels soft, like baby rabbit fur. According to Maureen, my partner, he doesn't respond to Titch and only answers when you call him Mr Titch.

Heidi, a tortoiseshell-coloured cat, is the grande dame of the house. She arrived as a brave little mother who was being fed by the next door neighbour because she had two boys who loved Heidi dearly. But when Heidi had kittens, she brought them to my house—even though I had a dog, the well-known Yoni. Heidi didn't really trust the boys with her three kittens and thought this was a safer household. She managed to live two lives, one in each house. But her first adopted mother didn't like or know anything about cats and wouldn't allow her into the house. She had Heidi spayed at my instigation but I had to take her to the vet to have her stitches removed. She kept one of the kittens, which was run over at two years old, and I found homes for the other two. Heidi made her choice and came to live with me because she could sit in front of the fire and on anyone's knee. What more could a cat want? She can look at anybody and make their heart melt. Still a young cat at seventeen, she's not very well at the moment but is holding her own in a household of strong cats.

Then there's Lucky, a fat tabby cat, who got his name because he was lucky. One evening, when he was still a kitten, he happened to be sitting by the side of the road, looking utterly lost and forlorn, when I was driving by on my way to an archives meeting. I immediately stopped and picked him up. The poor little thing was starving. I tried to find out who owned him but no one did, so I took him with me to the meeting, hoping someone else might take pity on him and adopt him. When that didn't happen he came home with me and he's been here ever since. Lucky by name and lucky by nature, that one.

As can be seen, three of the cats were kittens when I first met them and Heidi arrived with a litter of three. I think this explains why I have four cats. I adore kittens but kittens grow into cats and, as I take my responsibilities as a surrogate mother seriously, most of my cats make it into their twenties.

Thelma Solomon *became a political activist in 1969, when she chained herself to the Arbitration Court in protest at the inadequate representation of unions and the absence of ordinary womyn who were unable to put in submissions or speak on their own behalf at the equal pay hearings. In subsequent years, Thelma was involved in conferences and militant protests in many many areas, such as anti-beauty contests, equal opportunity for girls in schools, access to hotel bars, refuges for young womyn, health issues, lesbian political support groups, racism awareness, prostitution of womyn, lesbian businesses, collective film and video making and the Performing Older Women's Circus. Thelma died during the production of this book.*

Losing Familiars

Susan Wiseheart

I lived with Murranda, a small black cat, longer than anyone in my adult life except my children. Her hair was short and she had one white whisker. Her eyes were a penetrating yellow. She disdained direction and did what she wanted to do. She did not try to please but she was so beautiful it was inevitable. I remember her arranging herself on my lap, then settling into a curl with a sigh. All of her molecules sank into me and the most delightful energy drifted up from her small body.

One cold day in December, as I drove up a dirt road to work, a small tabby with a white chest and legs, a striped tail, blue eyes and lovely unique markings crawled into the sunlight on the road in front of my pick-up. 'That's my cat,' I thought.

Her head was huge, her body minuscule. She was starving. She was hypothermic. I stopped. She crawled under the truck. I coaxed and pulled her out and put her on the seat beside me. She was just under a year old and she was weak. Her back legs collapsed under her. The first night, she slept in bed with me, up close to my body heat. She was cold clear through.

Until I was sure she wasn't ill, she lived upstairs. I named her Sylvie. Every day, I went up several times to see her, holding her in my lap between my hands, petting and soothing her. I filled a bowl full to overflowing with food and I put echinacea in her water.

Murranda was distraught. Who was this interloper she could

smell but couldn't see, up in the space that used to be hers? When the day came for Sylvie to come downstairs, Murranda growled and spat. For months, she tried to drive Sylvie away. Up the stairs they'd go, Sylvie racing in fear, Murranda relentlessly chasing. Sylvie would dash as far as she could get into a corner, under the floorboards in a crawl space, hissing and yowling, facing off Murranda, who would eventually give up until the next time.

I was firm with them. I made mind pictures of them lying together in my lap, happy and calm. Eventually, it worked and they cuddled side by side. For a few more years, they were pals, sharing a basket in front of the stove in winter, grooming each other.

When she was only thirteen, Murranda became very ill. On her last day, I lay next to her on the couch, telling her as much of the story of her life as I knew and loving her.

The next day, she died from a needle. I drove her home from the vet, up and down the huge hills, crying hard. Digging a small round grave in a wild place in the garden, I placed her in it, curling her up in the same position she liked to take in my lap.

However, Murranda is still here. On a particular stretch of my morning walk, we often meet. She walks beside me, as high as my hand. She shrinks to the size of an ant. She grows as large to me as I was once to her, she the large human, and I the small cat. Other times, she is as big as a house, as big as a world. Then she slowly diminishes in size and I find myself inside her. I walk in her feet, see through her eyes. We grow smaller until we melt into the earth in a shining spot of energy and become the earth, spinning slowly through space, a fleck of the multiverse.

We sometimes ride together in my truck. She takes on the dimensions of a cocker spaniel, so it is easy for me to reach over, hold the nape of her neck, and stroke my hand along her spine to the end of her tail as she purrs her loud and rhythmic purr. The sound resonates through my body, the truck, the soil beneath the road, the planet.

Sometimes she merges with Sylvie. Sylvie used to be a silent kitty. Murranda was a gabber. Now that Murranda is no longer here in the physical, Sylvie has begun to talk more. It is Murranda, conversing through her. Sylvie houses her happily. I pet them both, running my hands along their full sides, delicately fingering each of their ears' tender edges. I smooth their faces, part their toes to massage the webs of their pads, and scratch softly under their chins, smiling and singing.

Susan Wiseheart lives on a Lesbian Land Trust in the Ozarks along with several other dykes, many domesticated and wild animals and plants, plus plenty of rocks. She loves water and has a special mission to work and play with it and care for it.

Eccentrics

Bronwyn Whitlocke

Over my fifty-odd years I have made the acquaintance of a number of cats but four stand out. They are special because of their idiosyncratic ways. Individuals from regal blood lines and moggies. Cats are independent, sometimes arrogant, and they definitely know what they want. So much like myself and what astrologers say about Aquarians, even a bit odd or eccentric. A cat is my familiar.

I have never gone looking for a cat but there has always been one in my life. Cats moved in with me by their choice; perhaps because they needed a home where they could live out their particular eccentricities. Or they came with a partner.

The love of my life was Zac, a silver tabby with a soft white smudge down his nose. As I sat in my kitchen one morning, I heard a thud on the back door. I ignored it, but then there was a second bump, like a soft body falling against something. This got me up. I opened the door and in walked, as if he already owned the place, a silver tabby. He strutted and strolled around the flat—all the while talking continuously. I guess I was being assessed. He received the obligatory bowl of milk almost immediately; within the week he had his personal water and food bowls.

Every evening, as I entered the flat, I was met with cat conversation. 'I have done this, I saw this, this happened, how was your day, where's my dinner, sit down—now! — and I'll sit on your lap and let you stroke me.' Zac slept on the bed, of course. I had to accept that, morning after morning, I would wake with a very soggy blanket which he had sucked during the night.

After five years I came home one night to no conversation. No Zac. I never saw him again. The word out in the neighbourhood was that cats were being nabbed for vivisection. I have always hoped he had adopted someone else.

My next feline acquaintance was a black Burmese named Mao (yes, as in Mao Tse Tung). He had been my mother's cat and I don't remember the reason why he became mine. He was huge, as big as a small dog. Equal in height to perhaps a bulldog. He was muscly and growled rather than meowed.

Along our back fence ran a lane and each morning Mao would sit on the fence and wait for the German shepherd's daily constitutional. His leaping on to the poor unsuspecting dog caused desperate yelps and screams, as the dog raced away. Next Mao would stroll in, obviously most satisfied with his tyranny.

Mao got a wire embedded in his jaw from the newspapers, that, in the sixties in Australia, were bound with wire. He came down with tetanus and lost the use of his back legs for a while but recovered and died, at the old age of twelve, peacefully in his sleep. My brave Mao.

Tiger, a little feral ginger tabby, was given to me by my sister. He had the unpleasant habit of sucking the hairs of the underarms of sleepers. After Tiger came to stay we acquired a German shepherd and a bull terrier. If either of them were on a lounge chair and Tiger walked in, both dogs would immediately get off and lay on the floor. Allowing his majesty to take the seat.

His forte (with apologies) was to occasionally kill a possum and leave its head on the front door mat. I never found the other body parts. The rosellas, though, had him stumped. I remember him sitting out on the porch, head down, tail swishing, crouched and ready to pounce. His quarry: a rosella. The bird, munching its seed, eyed Tiger. Then, slowly, the rosella strutted towards Tiger, pecked him on the head and flew off. Tiger shook his head and immediately fell off the rail he had been on. He died a natural death at the age of fourteen. That was Tiger.

Sam, a black moggie, came with my new partner. At our first meeting, he rubbed affectionately against my legs. I couldn't resist picking him up, he was so cuddly and cute. What a mistake! All four paws came out straight and were pushed against my chest; a cat with a personal space issue. I soon learnt that he was happy to be held with head and paws away from my body.

He had an endearing way of asking for food. Not much of a talker, he would use sign language. When he was hungry, he would first sit and stare at his bowl. If no food materialised, he would walk towards the cupboard which held his food. He would stretch up towards the cupboard and point with one outstretched paw to where he obviously knew the bounty was.

Sam was very Zen. If the door was closed, it meant he must go out; when the door was opened, it meant he must stay in. A totally independent and arrogant boy. It was his decision if he would give you the honour of sitting on your lap. No cajoling succeeded. Sam would often sit out in the garden, smelling flowers and mewling to the birds. The birds were safe from him.

Dear Sam succumbed to extreme diabetes and my partner made the unenviable decision to put him to rest. Goodbye, our panther Sam.

All my cats have been male; I wonder about that. Also, all my cats have been neutered; I wonder about that too.

Bronwyn Whitlocke is a Shiatsu therapist and Chinese Medicine Herbalist and acupuncturist in Melbourne with twenty years of professional and practical experience. She has always had cats and dogs in her life and currently lives with Max the Cat and Sophie the Dog. 🐾

Enlightenment from a Cat Born at the Lighthouse

Caz Brown

No home of mine enfolds me

or enriches my soul

without the presence

of a cat.

There have been many cats in my life. The first was a half-wild, black-and-white tom. I have few recollections of Whisk[e]y; know neither the correct spelling of his name nor whether he possessed a particularly Irish or Scottish temperament to match. Great Aunt Caroline called him Nervous Wreck. A mother's tale: he scratched me once—almost had my eye. Then there were the tortoiseshell shop-cats—the first cats my sister Pennie and I had the pleasure of naming, long before the Jellicle Cats with Jellicle Names had top billing. Years later, a friend begged me, packet of double-coated Tim Tams in hand, to adopt a collarless black-and-white cat who had chosen her workplace as a second home. I took one look at this cat, decided she looked like a Minnie Caldwell* cat in need of a Minnie Caldwell name… Queenie. Eventually this transmuted to Queenie Beanie, and then Beans.

But it was Thistle who was born at the lighthouse. She was my sister's Siamese cat and she emigrated with us from England, together with Lady (our Dobermann) and Mo (my grandmother's poodle). We were a living cliché—English and totally dotty about our animals. When we received our emigration approval papers, animals weren't being let into Australia. We were about to turn down the offer, but within a matter of days the ban was lifted.

And so the adventure began. Lady, Mo and Thistle had to travel to Tilbury by train, alone in the guard's van, the dogs muzzled and the cat in a carry box. Thistle ended up travelling the next day because she succeeded in fighting her way out of a sturdy orange box. Box number two was solid timber with rope handles and air holes. They were to sail ahead of us on a cargo ship. Australian quarantine lasted six months and, for the dogs, the boat trip counted towards this because they did not touch land during their voyage. Thistle, however, was mistakenly set ashore at Adelaide and had to travel by rail to Melbourne, so her sentence had to recommence on arrival at the Spotswood Quarantine Centre. Lady arrived very thin, despite having been adopted by one of the sailors and sleeping in his cabin; Mo was having a very woolly hair day; and Thistle, not

---

* Minnie Caldwell and Ena Sharples were from the cast of 'Coronation Street': they were two old spinsters who drank together in the Rovers Return.

having seen the light of day, looked as if she had been up a chimney, albeit a brown-sooted one. Her coat never regained that palest cream background, perfection for her seal-coloured points.

Aged thirteen, my enlightenment began. My sister was gradually acquiring more and more animals—the beginning of her lifelong passion. Teenage judgement is harsh and often unjust. I felt Thistle was being abandoned and, in a none-too-subtle way, befriended her. Or perhaps, being a cat, it was she who did the befriending. We shared Cornflakes swimming in milk at the breakfast table; greetings after being parted; armchairs in the evenings (although her favourite sleeping spot was on top of the television, tail dangling mid-screen); and a bed at night. I would sleep foetal-position and Thistle would sleep under the covers, curled up next to my belly. I would wake up in the middle of the night and place my hand on her to check if she was still breathing, afraid she would suffocate, or that I would accidentally roll onto her. She was my confidante.

I was eighteen when Thistle died. I was out dancing at a nightclub—Bombay Rock in Brunswick—with a couple of friends. Suddenly, and without warning, I bent over, a severe pain in my belly for which there was no explanation—my period wasn't due, I didn't have food poisoning. When I arrived home, I found Mum's note pinned to the front door… they'd had to take Thistle to the vet's and he was keeping her there. The vet had had to syringe fluid from Thistle's lungs, which was a painful procedure, and it seemed that this had happened at exactly the same time as my pain. Telepathic empathy?

Details of Thistle's illness are hazy—I think she had pulmonary pneumonia. Anyway, there was no doubt she would have to be put to sleep. I rang the vet and was both shocked and furious when he suggested that I need not be present. He didn't know me and must have presumed I would cause a fuss. Upset as I was, I refused to abandon her. Dad drove me to the surgery and I spent a few minutes with her. She purred the whole time. The vet said this was a normal reaction to help breathing in a cat with this illness. Calmly, I held her while he administered the injection. We wrapped her in a towel and took her home. Her shroud should have been silk.

Caz Brown is a Melbourne designer who shares her life with Keiko, Lulu and Queenie aka Beans, their Guardian Angel Cat (whose ashes live on top of the fridge in a black-and-white, cat-shaped ceramic biscuit barrel). She has a BA in Writing and Literature, aspires to being fluent in cat language and wishes she could purr. 🐾

In the Year of the Cat

Susan Hawthorne

I was born in the year of the cat. You'd have thought that would bring me lots of luck with cats. But the luck is fickle. And loyalty is difficult.

The farm I grew up on had once been home to twenty-six cats. That was before my parents married. My mother could not abide living with so many cats (understandably because she was born in the year of the rat). So they were shot. Twenty-five of them. Only one remained. He was a ginger called either Marmalade or Ginger and his presence coincides with my life for just a few thin years.

I did not have another encounter with a cat of any significance until I was fourteen. Even though kittens continued to be born on our farm, they always disappeared before we children could locate the source of their mewling.

When I was fourteen and at boarding school, a white cat set up house in our bedroom. The doctor's daughter noticed that she was pregnant. She was the same girl, who upon learning her cat had died just before going away to school, insisted she needed the comfort of her cat's fur. What had once been a cat was now a large black furry mitten. I felt squeamish putting my hand into the inside-out cat.

One morning we woke to a hoarse and painful miaow and blood on our bedspreads. From 5 to 7 a.m. the four of us attended in awe as nine kittens were born. We watched as White Cat licked the sac and ate the placentas, and our hands were tempted to reach out to help the squirming wet bundles to the teat. But once again the doctor's daughter said, 'No, she won't bond if you touch them.' It was a Sunday and we had to go to mandatory church. So we set up a nest behind the drawers in the fireplace, a secure and warm spot, and left hoping that mother and kittens would remain quietly for the next two hours. We walked back from church so fast that day and upon returning, barricaded ourselves against the pursuing crowd and pressed another set of drawers up against the door of our bedroom.

I don't know who spread the news, but within minutes a crowd of teenage girls were banging on the door of our room. One said, 'I'm going to be a nurse; I have to learn about the sight of blood.' We knew it would not be long before the house mistress would come asking what all the ruckus was about. And come she did. 'What's going on?' 'Nothing,' came the limp reply. At which point the kittens resumed their high-pitched chorus. The drawers were pulled forward and White Cat and her kittens were exposed only to be banished to the care of old Mrs McDonald who lived on site with her caretaker husband. We had visiting rights, but it wasn't the same as having a family of cats in your bedroom. Our interest waned within a week.

Within a couple of years of leaving school, I adopted a stray black cat who was wild through and through. She scavenged and scratched but we reached an amicable agreement eventually. I always thought she would disappear as suddenly as she had appeared. It was worse than that. She was run over, dragged herself back to me and then had to be put down. In the end it was she who was more loyal than me.

Soon after, Puss came into my life. A beautiful fluffy tortoiseshell with a personality that was always on edge. She jumped when she saw her reflection in the mirror. She scratched when she was picked up, but if she decided it suited her, she would sit heavily on your lap and then pound her paws endlessly. One night she found herself caught on the windowsill outside my bedroom one floor up. She'd walked along the sill, but could not turn. It was quite a drop to the ground. I tried to convince her to back towards me so I might grab her, but even if she had, she was too far away. Eventually I went downstairs and stood on the lawn calling her. After some baulking and several false starts she proved her amazing intelligence by sliding down the concrete wall and leaping out to the lawn at a jumpable height.

Puss and I lived together through some tumultuous life-changing times over about five or six years. She was my point of stability. But it was the next cat, another stray, Lysippe, named after an Amazon queen, who stayed the longest. Lysippe was a sweet-natured friendly cat without the personality idiosyncracies of her predecessors. She shared her life with me and Puss for a time, but outgrew us both. Lysippe loved to burrow down into the bedclothes and curl around my feet. Sometime during the night it would get too stuffy down there and she'd emerge to wheeze somewhere near my ear.

When my blue heeler dog joined us around 1981 as a puppy, I tried to convince Lysippe that she should get in and boss Miles around while she had the size advantage. But she didn't and wouldn't. When Miles grew much bigger than her, Lysippe would allow Miles to roll in the sun near her in mock fight mode. She never did get to be boss of the household, except for the few times when she was sole proprietor.

Lysippe had started out as my partner's cat in 1974, accompanied the two us through several houses until we parted, and then Lysippe moved in to my house. She stayed and comforted me, wheezing through many long nights while I wrestled with an unsettled and uncertain life until the next long-term relationship. When the relationship finished, Lysippe stayed on with that partner. She, as it turned out, was the mistress of loyalty and longevity. She died of old age at seventeen years.

Susan Hawthorne writes poetry, fiction and non-fiction and regularly indulges in her passion for aerials and performance in circus. She avoids movies about animals because they make her cry too much. She is currently writing about the inspirational value of lesbian culture and the dissonances between patriotism and feminism.

Feline Friends

Kate Munro

Sexy, sassy, attention-seeking and neurotically housebound, her name was Madeleine and she was part of a package deal offered to me as an attractive house-sitting arrangement on Vancouver Island. I accepted, we bonded and I was forevermore hooked on the idiosyncrasies of Abyssinians. Folk frequently remark that 'Abbies' are more like dogs than cats. They're wrong. Although Abbies will fetch a ball and come when you whistle, they seduce and subdue you with the sinuous stealth peculiar to cats.

On my return to Australia, I resolved to search for an Abby of my own. For my first ever pet I wanted a smart *prima donna* with attitude. When I found her, I knew immediately that we would make a memorable team. She was mischief itself, a ruddy red Abby with a cheeky face and a heart that knew no fear. I called her 'Greer' and no doubt her namesake would have been equally enchanted.

On Christmas day when she was a mere ten weeks old, she scampered around everyone's feet in the kitchen making a serious nuisance of herself. In the midst of the bustle I noticed that she had disappeared. Residents and guests alike, all hunted inside and out for the wayward kitten. Alas, there was no sign of her and I was close to tears at the prospect of losing my wee friend. My friend, ever ready with a consoling 'cuppa' sat me down in the kitchen and put the kettle on. Opening the fridge door to get the milk, she stood frozen—there, sitting on the very crowded top shelf of the fridge, was Greer, shivering and clearly keen to get out but seemingly no worse for wear. No one has any idea how long she spent in the fridge, or indeed how she got in there, but there was general consensus that she had used the first of her 'lives' that morning!

This was by no means the only time she tempted fate. Another memorable incident saw her retreat almost to the top of a forty-metre river gum after being chased by a German shepherd tethered to its base. Greer remained there for five days before anyone knew of her whereabouts and was able to organise an adventurous and foolhardy climber to rescue her.

Her most endearing episode occurred when we were visiting my parents. Knowing the risks for her in a strange neighbourhood, my father set up a 'run' so that she might wander within the garden. Apart from the inevitably tangled consequences of tying a cat to anything, nobody factored in the temptation of the fishpond with the flickering gold flashes of fish gliding by. Greer perched herself on the edge of the pond for quite some time, alternating between appearing to be intensely interested and arrogantly indifferent. In the midst of our family barbeque, without warning, Greer dived headlong into the pond in pursuit of her own gourmet dinner. It is difficult to know who was the most alarmed, and Greer never ventured near it again, though she demonstrated little fear of water for the rest of her life.

Greer came to an untimely end when a car hit her. I recall the intensity of the grief as I sat in the gutter and bawled like a baby in gasping sobs that crushed my chest and burnt my throat as the tears tumbled forth.

It was not until several years later that I dared consider the possibility of another cat. Again I opted for the cheeky charms of an Abyssinian male with inordinately large ears. His name is Mr Spock and though he lacks Greer's 'attitude', he is affectionate and loyal. Like Greer he was fearless as a kitten, roaming freely during daylight hours through the many acres of bushland in our riverfront home with his neighbourhood feline friends.

His principal failing is that he is a shamefully quick hunter, bringing home all manner of prey including, to my despair, various species of wildlife, both feathered and furry. Amid

his terrible tally have been five sizable snakes, two of which were very much alive and none too impressed at being dumped on my lounge-room floor. His other more engaging but nonetheless troublesome flaw was to follow me to the bus stop most mornings. No matter how loudly I stood at the corner and stamped my foot, growled, threw stones or yelled at him he would resume stalking me to within metres of the main road. It seemed to be his morning sport and I lived in fear that his wilfulness would lead him to the same fate as Greer.

When we moved to a more suburban setting, Mr Spock was locked inside for most of the day and night and initially showed all the signs of being depressed, neurotic, bored and above all lonely. There was only one solution for it: a playmate.

This time I opted to visit my local RSPCA and there, sitting waiting for me, was a strikingly exotic charcoal Shorthair. This kitten had the largest, most piercing and alert green eyes I had ever seen. When I decided to take him, the attendant informed me that he was born on 11 September 2001. On the spot, and in the best of taste, I decided to call him Osama. It was a prophetic choice as this cat has the same spirit and capacity to evade capture as his namesake. After a period of intense rivalry, he and Mr Spock settled into an uneasy but respectful truce as equals, sleeping on opposite corners of the foot of my bed each night. However, in the best tradition of Abyssinian audacity, on cold winter nights it is Mr Spock who can be found between the sheets, asleep with his head on the pillow beside me.

Kate Munro is a feminist and public sector manager. After providing a home to her first cat, Kate came to truly understand the notion that 'dogs have owners and cats have staff'. Kate now endures a life of servitude in Brisbane with her two cats, Osama and Mr Spock.

Christie Our Black (and White) Cat

Emma Inturatana Rice and Pranee Liamputtong

Cats! When Pranee was young, having a cat as a best friend and as a pet was not in her mind! This is her story.

I grew up in Thailand where children were told many myths about cats, particularly black cats. There is something mysterious about them. When Thai people talk about cats, they are drawn to think about death, ghosts and evil spirits.

I remembered hearing stories about a black cat jumping across a coffin. It was feared that this act would awaken the dead person and (s)he would then be able to haunt and harm people who were still alive! This was a warning not to let a black cat near a coffin at a funeral.

A funeral in Thai culture takes several days. There will always be people guarding coffins, day and night as Thai people believe that prior to reincarnation, the dead should not return to life. If they do, they are destined to turn into fearsome ghosts.

As death has a lot to do with spirits who roam in the human world, Thai children have great fears about deceased people, ghosts and spirits. These are all called 'phi' in Thai. It is thought that they can punish people for offences committed against them. Punishments may result in sicknesses or death. Black cats always appear in any story about ghosts and spirits.

All Thai children will learn the fearsome legend of Nang Nak Pra Khanong. The legend was made into a movie. A new version about Nang Nak was shown at the Melbourne Film Festival. Nang Nak was a young and beautiful woman, who resided in the Pra Khanong district. She died in childbirth while her beloved husband, Mak, was at the war which Siam (now Thailand) was waging against the Burmese.

When Mak returned he was weak and ill, so Nang Nak appeared as a human being to take care of him. Mak later discovered that she was now a spirit. He sought refuge in a monastery as she would not be able to take him with her (meaning he would die). It is believed that spirits are unable to enter a sacred ground of a monastery. Nang Nak was unable to relinquish her love for Mak, and she begged him to return. He refused. This made Nang Nak sad and angry. She manifested as a fearsome spirit and killed many of those who opposed her. During all these horrific scenes, black cats appeared. Their screeching sounds and big red eyes made everyone jump. This is why Thai children fear black cats!

As an adult living in Melbourne and with two children who love cats, my attitude towards cats has changed a great deal. I had good neighbours who loved their two Siamese cats. Coco was a pure white cat while Nanky was yellowish-brown. Every day these cats came to my house for extra feeds. Both would eat my left-over food; even some of my Thai food which was bit spicy. My children, Zoe and Emma, loved to cuddle and play with them. I have a picture in my mind of Zoe when she first learned to sit. I saw her reach out to pat Coco. This made me think that cats were not so bad after all. Cats, perhaps, can be friends.

Then, one day they found Christie, a black-and-white cat. And now here is Emma's story.

Christie, our cat, had a bad life before she came to our home. Her owners were known to hit her and torture her. But just as well, Christie has come to our house where I treasure her as one of the family. The story of Christie was very queer but this was the way it went. A long time ago, there was a cat that always came around to our house at night. We called her Christie and we fed her scraps and she ate anything including Mum's rice.

One night, she disappeared and has never returned. Mum took me and my sister, Zoe, to the RSPCA. 'Just to have a look at the cats,' Mum told us. Then a black-and-white cat happened to come up to us. It affectionately smoothed its face on our hands. We fell in love with the cat. Zoe and I pleaded and so Mum gave in and we ended up getting her. We named her Christie, just the same as the other cat that we lost.

Our first point of view of this cat was that she would eat anything, just like Christie number one. But, no, Christie number two just has to be so choosy. She would not eat Mum's scraps. Worse still, she is so picky with her toilet stuff. If her cat tray is a bit smelly (because she has done it once) she would just do it on the bathroom floor. This drives Mum nuts. Many times, Mum had to get up at night to clean up the toilet because she could not tolerate the mess Christie had done. But Christie is one of my best friends and we love her.

So a cat is in our life now! Having had a negative attitude toward cats in my childhood, one might wonder how I can have a cat in my life, particularly, as Emma points out, one that drives me crazy. Well! She is a black-and-white cat. Maybe it is not so bad and fearful after all!

Emma was born in Melbourne in 1991. She is in Grade 6 at Mont Albert Primary School. She loves animals, but particularly cats, dogs and horses. She takes lessons in violin, flute and recorder. She is in her school's orchestra, concert band, a recorder consortium and choir. Her ambition is to have her own pets one day.

Pranee was born in 1955 in Thailand. She lived and was educated in Thailand until she received a scholarship to undertake her doctoral degree at Monash University. She has been living in Melbourne since 1983. She is at present an associate professor in the School of Public Health, La Trobe University. In addition to her academic work (teaching, researching and publishing), Pranee enjoys embroidering, gardening and cooking. Pranee has two daughters, Zoe and Emma.

Cats in Drag and Other Felines*

Bronwyn Winter

I was brought up with dogs. They were always part of my life. Part of my family. Cats came into my life much later—and of course they changed it, as cats are wont to do.

I have a photograph of me at the age of three with a cross labrador/cocker spaniel protectively planted in front of me, looking suspiciously at the camera. And so it went on through my childhood—dogs that seemed to want to protect me against the world. Dogs are like that.

No cats. My father didn't like cats. So we didn't have cats.

And then along came Anna. Anna was a black cat with a white chest and white bits on her face and the occasional white paw. My first cat. My first Very Own Cat. (Or rather, the first cat to Very Own Me.) I was eighteen and Anna was an ageing kitten, a stray that some kind person had nurtured and given to me. Some months later, along came the blue heeler/kelpie cross: my first very own Cat In Drag. With the ridiculous name of Wocket (after the Dr Seuss book *There's a Wocket in my Pocket* because as an eight-week-old puppy she fitted into the pocket of my big beige winter jacket). Anna used to sit up on the wall of the house I co-inhabited in Rozelle, and would divebomb Wocket as she was puppy-prancing about in the front garden. Wocket thus

developed a very healthy respect for Anna. Anna was The Boss. Anna was My Cat. And She Came First.

Anna also seduced my father. My father who hated cats. I once stayed with my parents in between houses, with Anna, and the then *two* cats-in-drag: Wocket, now somewhat too large to fit in even the biggest of my pockets, and Scruffy, aptly named, a scruffy nondescript sort of terrier stray that friends had rescued and bestowed upon me as a collector of All Things Animalian.

My father had a gammy leg (from a road accident many years earlier). He also had a tendency towards gout in his good leg. And by the time I, and my cat Anna, and my two cats-in-drag arrived to stay (although only Scruffy really claimed any sort of Catness: terriers can be pretentious that way), my father was seventyish. So getting on a bit. I was twentyish.

Dad had a comfy chair with attendant footstool. It was his place. Where he sat. Where he put his tired old legs to rest. Anna, the day we moved in, had looked at my father and said to herself: 'Right, so you think you don't like cats? We'll see about that.' And she quite deliberately set out to seduce him. By the time I moved out again a few weeks later, Anna was not only curling up on Dad's lap without the slightest protest from him,

---

* The title of this piece comes from Renate Klein. I missed the deadline for the now celebrated dog book, so I asked if I could perhaps write about my dogs as well for the cat book, as cats and dogs (raining or otherwise) both seem constantly to people—or rather, animal—my life. Renate promptly responded with the title 'cats in drag'. So Cats In Drag it is.

but when she was in his chair, he would go and sit somewhere else Because He Couldn't Possibly Disturb Anna. His place was Her Place. Simple as that. She had won my father's unconditional love (as cats will insist on doing—but beware of ever asking for it back!). Had succeeded in making him understand that Only Cats Really Count.

Someone once told me that if you rub butter on a cat's paws they will be yours for life (because they will lick off the butter and your scent and taste with it). I don't remember if I ever rubbed butter on Anna's paws. But she was My Cat. Even long after I had gone to live in Europe, and Anna had taken up residence with some nice people in the Blue Mountains, she remained My Cat. I went to visit, hadn't seen her for some years, and she literally ran into my arms. My First Cat Love. And Dad was her person.

The most intense cat relationship I have had has been with Gertrude. Gertrude was the darkest darkest tortoiseshell, with a light ginger patch over one eye that made her look either cross or extremely surprised. Or perhaps, to combine the two, somewhat affronted. She sought out small safe spaces and held my current two cats-in-drag, Hector and Sarafina, in complete awe. They are hardly your Wilting Violet (or Cringing Cur) sort of dogs, but they used to tippytoe around Gertrude. Gertude was your Original Scary Cat.

Gertrude was also the World's Most Neurotic Cat. She claimed affection, imperiously and immediately, but would bite the hand that caressed her. She would curl up on your lap and purr, and her tail would be waving about and beating an impatient rhythm on your belly.

Gertrude was already affronted as a kitten. You just knew not to mess with her. Two of my earliest memories of Gertrude are of her attacking the

back of a couch, a wild wild (and most affronted) look in her eyes, and hissing at herself in the mirror (even more affronted). A third memory is of her curled up in an impossibly tiny flowerpot, staring (most affrontedly) at me saying, 'Whaddayamean, this pot's too small?'

Gertrude ended up being terribly stressed by Life, the Universe and Everything. She took to overgrooming her belly red raw. And in the end died of kidney failure. She was extremely high maintenance, a very demanding cat. But so terribly interesting. Smart, very smart. I cried a river of tears at her passing. I was Gertrude's Person.

__Bronwyn Winter__ grew up with dogs and embraced cats somewhere along the way (as one does). She speaks both dog and cat fluently and her cat friends, being rather talented individuals (as they are), speak excellent French. Bronwyn is also co-editor of Spinifex's September 11, 2001: Feminist Perspectives.

My Life, My Love, My Art, My Cats

Cheryl Osborne

Ever since I was a little girl, I have always loved cats. They have been essential, if not quintessential, to my life. I have only lived without a cat on two very short occasions. Cats have been my focus in my life and art.

Giselle, named after the ballet, was the first cat to feature in my painting. A white cat, with golden eyes and a soft nature, who sometimes shed a tear. When the vet told us she could get skin cancer in her pink shell ears, my mother put a sunshade in the garden for her. This became 'Cat under a Sunshade'. A brightly coloured fauve cat in an exotic garden, sitting under a sunshade. This was one of my first of many cat paintings. These paintings are symbolic and narrative.

One day I found Amari in a fish shop. She was a smudgy apricot-and-white stripey kitten. The day before I had bought an Imari cat. The man in the antique shop thought it was an Amari cat. As T S Eliot said, 'the Naming of Cats is a difficult matter.' Thus she was named or misnamed. As it turned out, the Amari cat was, in fact, an Imari cat, a china pillow used by The Emperors and decorated with dragons.

Amari's feisty nature was evident from the start. She owned me and I loved her with all my heart. In 1990, I spent five weeks travelling in France. I missed Amari and imagined she was with me. This developed into my series of French cat paintings. 'Two Cats on the Beach at Nice', a large oil painting depicting Amari licking her Drumstick and a French Feline Friend sipping a cup of café crème. I was the girl with the yellow upturned hairdo. She and a Siamese Tourist Cat climbed the Eiffel Tower. She walked with me in the forest at Chateau Brecourt, a castle owned by one of the King Louises near Giverney. These paintings and others were exhibited at a gallery owned by two Burmese cat lovers. Cat people always find one another.

When my marriage ended, I returned to my parents' home and Amari became the fifth cat in a house of three humans. My parents always have the correct perspective on life. Giselle already had a friend, a seven-eighths Tonkinese named Mazurka, after the dance. Saskia was a Calico cat named after Rembrandt's wife. Sebastian, a black cat with white whiskers, eye lashes, paws and a dinner shirt was named after that incorrigible character in 'Brideshead Revisited'. He and Amari fell in love and this resulted in a series of paintings about lovers. They went on candlelight dinner dates; they met secretly in the atrium. They did all the things lovers do.

My mother died of cancer in 1995 and I remembered how she had put out the sunshade to protect Giselle. She was given three months to live and lived another twenty-one years. Perhaps there was a sunshade protecting her too.

Amari and I moved into our own home in the following year. She even had her own answering machine. She sent me off to school each day saying, 'I got it right in this incarnation. Last time I was a teacher, now I am a higher being. You go out and pay the mortgage and look after me.' I realised why the ancient Egyptians made cats their gods.

In September 1999, I was stroking Amari and found a lump. My cat-specialist vet rang me and told me she had an incurable type of cancer. I had a terrible sense of déjà vu. We did all we could. In hope, she had three operations. A vet naturopath visited her at home and gave her her own flower essences. One Saturday, in June 2000, she became an Angel Cat. As I had done with my mother, I memorialised her in a painting.

In January 2000, I fractured my left knee. Amari cared for me as I did for her. When she went to heaven, I felt that I would not be able to have another cat as my mobility is limited. Suddenly I remembered my mother bringing home my first kitten as a box of medicine to cure the measles. Eighteen months later I ventured to the Cat Protection Society one Sunday morning. I had been a director of this society in the late 1980s and early 1990s. I immediately fell in love with small, fluffy kitten with eye makeup and a dappled white, gold, caramel and dark brown fur coat. I named her Camille after Monet's wife. I then saw a reincarnation of Sebastian, a very timid boy cat. I named him Sancho after Don Quixote's Sancho Panza. Now the answering machine is theirs. Like Amari they always choose the gifts for their mother. I have already painted their portraits, and a painting of them playing in the garden. They are still young and playful and dream of catching the birds and butterflies. Their cat pole dominates the living room. They too own me. The ancient Egyptians would be pleased.

Confucius once said, 'Never trust a man who doesn't like a cat.' I believe in what this great philosopher said; cats are central to my life. I adore and love them. I cannot live without a cat or two. Yes, they really are 'my life, my love, my art.'

A tribute to all the cats I have loved, and the cats I have yet to love.

Cheryl Osborne is an artist who includes a cat in almost every painting she paints. She went to art school from 1977-1983. She has exhibited widely, including one show in Singapore. At the moment, she shares her life with two cats.

The Family Kittens and Cats Alexandra Rees

My cats were special to me. They only went near me, nobody else, not even my mum or dad. I love cats and kittens. Marbles was the naughty one because she scratched the car and Patty was the grumpy one because she was always grumpy with everyone and everything. Marbles had to go to a cats' home because she kept killing all the birds and Patty ran away soon after. I hadn't seen Patty for about two years but one day I saw her in the driveway of the nearby neighbour's house. I called her but she just walked away. I was so sad.

Before Patty ran away and Marbles went to a cats' home, we were so close to each other. Even my dog Bouffy loved Marbles and Patty. I loved them so much. When I was little I said I was running away and I took Marbles and Patty with me. I only walked up the street and came back. I didn't really run away. I was too scared.

I was also close to my Aunty Rose's cat Ruby. She was a beautiful black cat but she was never close to me. Ruby was a real mummy's girl. But she was still a beautiful cat. I loved her as much as Marbles and Patty. I got Marbles from my Aunty Nicole because she couldn't look after her. So she became my cat. I got Patty from Little Babcia. (Little Babcia is my Great Grandma. I call my Grandma Big Babcia. I just have, ever since I can remember. Babcia is Polish for Grandmother.) When Patty was a kitten she was thrown in my Babcia's backyard. So Babcia rang my mum and said, 'Do you want a cat?' My Mum said, 'Yes!' So that's how I got Patty. Little Babcia still has one of Patty's kittens. Her name is Suzie and she's about ten years old now. In my family, kittens always get shared around.

My dad saved Ruby from a gutter one night when it was pouring with rain. She had a sister with her but Dad couldn't get that one. Mum says that Ruby was a wild cat, flinging herself all over the car and scratching her everywhere. They decided to give Ruby to my aunty. When I was three I used to try and pat Ruby but she'd run away. Then I would cry and say, 'Aunty Rose, why does she run away from me? I'm just a kid.' My Aunty Rose's first very own cat was one of Marbles' kittens. It was a boy she named Gabriel. Gabriel ran away too. That was when I was a baby.

I miss Patty and Marbles. I am hoping to get two more cats because I love them. I think my two-year-old sister Layla would love them too. I love cats and kittens. Do you?

Alexandra Edith Rees is ten years old. Her birthday is 17 March 1993. She loves all sorts of animals. She loves dancing, singing and eating too. Her three favourite hobbies are drawing, collecting Hello Kitty and writing stories. She hopes you enjoyed her story about cats.

From Eric

Barbara Becker, Jan Weate & Sal Hampson

Three women loved me. I have to say them alphabetically or they might think I'm picking favourites. Barbara, Jan and Sal.

What individual personalities they have and, of course, I had a different relationship with each of them. Barbara is great; after all, she gave me my name. She was such a softy with me; if I hid under the bed or bath, she'd let me stay in all day—no problem! She didn't like me stretching out in her arms—how weird is that! But she made me so proud when she told everyone how clever I was, how I knew which way all the doors opened but I wouldn't exert myself if one of them would open the door for me—got to save all that energy for more interesting things I reckoned! Her favourite story was the time I entertained all three of them by working out how to get a squash ball out of a cardboard box. That was fab. I thought about it a lot to be honest, how to get that ball out. I rolled it into the corner of the box, me standing on the outside, hooked my paw underneath and slowly, slowly lifted it up. The bugger would nearly get to the top but every time it rolled over my paw and fell back down. Well, I walked round and round that box, thinking all the time then, that was it… I slapped the box, it fell over and the ball rolled out—wow, what a moment, it took loads of self-control not to run around celebrating but I didn't, I just walked off, just like that, problem solved!

Now Jan; there's another story and one that happened a long time ago. Jan was around when I was very small. She used to spend loads of time with me, telling me how beautiful I was and giving me cuddles. I don't know why, but I had a thing about soft toys, you know, the things little kids have. Anyway, in Jan's room there was this great window, right out onto the roof. I could get out there and

go into pretty well any house on the street. I sussed out the ones with the kids and I used to spend ages in there choosing a favourite toy. It had to have a bit of something, but it took me a while to work out what. I started a bit big and that was down to Jan. She had this teddy—a big brown thing—about four times the size of me, but I got that bear and dragged it all the way downstairs, and heaved it bodily through the heavy door into Sal's room—it made Jan and Sal laugh so much, they thought I was just the best. After that it was easy, white rabbit (in a frock), bulldog, polar bear, fluffy dice, wow, what a jamboree! They even bought me my own pig. Jan got me sorted around dogs too. She used to go round to this other house and I didn't fancy being left on my own so I'd follow her, even on the main road. She never tried to stop me, it was a great adventure, and when we got there, there was this other cat, a bit woossy and not good on conversation, but also this huge dog—I conquered that pretty quickly.

Sal was different again; it's amazing really, just how different they are. What to say about Sal. Well, she had this thing where she would hold me upside down in her arms (she didn't mind stretching), and she'd blow a great big raspberry on my belly. I never did let her know I wanted to giggle. I'd let her do it a couple of times then I had to make her stop so I'd curl back up and bite her on the nose—and what a nose, it was great, it stuck out like nothing else, just there waiting for me to chomp it! Then she'd be the mean one, never would let me stay in on a work day but I didn't mind really, I liked being outside. And that's where I am now, perpetually outside. They gave me a good send off and I have a great view.

And me, well, I have been a very lucky cat. When I talked to, and played and sometimes fought with the strays around here, I always had a warm home to go back to where I could stretch out, and when they put that fire on, I would rest my chin on the hearth. The strays used to come in the kitchen window and steal my food, I didn't ever stop them, I thought the least I could do was help them out in that little way—hey, that's just me!

Eric the Bold, RIP, 1994–2002.

Sal Hampson and *Barbara Becker* *live, work and play in West Yorkshire, England but dream of a place in France where Sal can write to her heart's content and Barbara can cycle up Pyrenean mountains. They shared their home with Eric until Christmas 2002 and have recently adopted a girl cat in her dotage, fourteen year old Maisie-Gray.* *Jan Weate*, *Sal and Eric shared a student household in Bradford, West Yorkshire. Jan is now an excited member of Performing Older Womens Circus in Melbourne where she is okay as long as she keeps away from the baked beans and fried onions. She also loves to cross-country ski, and has a fluffy, forgetful young pussycat called Delia.* 🐾

Section Three CATastrophes

The Life of Brian and Badger

Sandy Jeffs

Brian was a big, beefy, black cat. Quite majestic really. He was purportedly half-Siamese. He possessed the imperial lines of a true regal feline—long elegant black legs, exotic face and eyes that sparkled like gold. Brian was young, in the prime of his life and full of health and vigour. He was also an idiot. He would often sleep on the mantelpiece and languidly roll over only to find himself uncontrollably falling. He would desperately try to save himself and, in doing so, leave huge scratch marks on the wood. It was a nice piece of furniture before Brian. There was no end to his stupidity. He was also a projectile spewer for most of his life, something that was, frankly, unattractive and unpleasant.

This time of our lives was also shared with another cat, Badger, a gentlemen in every sense of the word. He was black and white and his markings made him look as though he was wearing a tuxedo, something I always thought was every way appropriate for such a dignified and charming character. Badger was ageing gracefully and at seventeen was in the twilight of his life. He always offered the paw of friendship to any new animal we brought into the household, including Brian. After the feral cat incident he may have regretted his accommodating gesture.

It began inauspiciously. We heard the odd spat and cat's yowl thinking it might have been a tit for tat between the two boys. And as it seemed very close by, like on our back verandah, we weren't concerned. However, over the course of a couple of days, it became clear there was a rather ferocious feral cat stalking our house and picking fights with our boys. Brian and Badger retreated to the house, clearly terrified by this bully from the bush. The feral cat was a brazen thing coming right up to the back door and yowling with a bloodcurdling sound that made even us scared of its presence.

It seems Brian made a decision that something had to be done. This feral intruder had to be dealt with. Someone had to make a stand. Brian placed himself on the bench in the kitchen where the food was served, from which he had spewed many times and from which he was going to co-ordinate the war with the feral cat. Being the supreme tactician, he decided to deploy his troop, saying to Badger, 'I'll hold the fort in here, you go outside and deal with the feral cat.' Badger, taking his duties very seriously, went outside and began his campaign that was doomed before it had even started. He fought heroically even though the feral cat was twice his size and full of fight. Badger sustained quite a few injuries. He had lost the battle and suffered immeasurably, while Brian, who had had a very stressful time on the bench, survived the day, intact.

About two days after the incident, we noticed Badger darting in and out of the pantry. He would dart behind the chair, then dart back into the pantry. He was acting as though something was stalking him, as though he was being persecuted and pursued by some ghostly demon. He looked totally unhinged. He looked like he was hearing voices and hallucinating. His little eyes were bulging and looked crazed. His behaviour was erratic and he was unable to relax or eat or purr. This went on for a few days and we became concerned. I had seen similar types of behaviour in the various nut houses I had been in myself. I had seen those eyes before and was convinced something was not quite right.

Worried, I took Badger to the vet. I described Badger's behaviour and mentioned the fight with the feral cat. The vet took one look at his eyes and concluded Badger was suffering from Post-Traumatic Stress Disorder! He *was* temporarily mad and needed treatment for the symptoms. Badger was given medication and orders to relax. We brought him home and gave him all the attention we could. He had been the bravest boy. Brian had not noticed anything. He was still on the bench when Badger came home and remained there for the next twelve years eating and spewing. Bravery was not really Brian's thing. He was always the self-interested one, unlike Badger who oversaw his household with assiduous care.

The feral cat did meet its demise. We intervened and disposed of it, allowing Badger to once again have his home and health and a place from which to extend his paw of feline friendship. Badger was loved by all and will always be remembered for his heroics and gentleness. Brian, on the other hand, wasn't everyone's favourite, but he did have some redeeming features, though I struggle to identify them. But I loved him with a passion. I was the only person in the world who loved him. Perhaps it was a meeting of two outcasts. I can still see him sitting on the bench miaowing for food and projectile spewing with a gay abandon in a way only he could. We always thought of him as a high class alley cat without the prowess of one who could survive the rough and tumble of the alley. He wasn't meant for that, he was meant to live on the bench, with Badger protecting him. For Brian, life was meant to be easy, even if it was at the expense of Badger's sanity!

Sandy Jeffs *has shared her life with many cats over the years who have given her much pleasure and enriched her life immeasurably. She presently lives with Neville and Gerald, two gay Burmese boys, and Ruby, a gorgeous cattle dog. Sandy has had four books of poetry published dealing with madness, domestic violence and midweek ladies tennis. She lives with her friends on the outskirts of Melbourne.*

Ralphie Boy

Jan Thorburn

Ralphie Boy was not the sort of cat a feminist should have, really. He was a dour, sour and fierce pussy. He'd take a swipe at you as soon as look at you. He always appeared to be searching for someone or something to sink his claws into. There was a constant, restless roving in his eye, a constant, restless twitching in his clawed paw.

The woman I lived with at the time I had Ralphie Boy had a little dog—a loveable little thing with floppy ears and a swirly, fluffy tail. The dog's name was Lo tse which was apparently Tibetan for 'little piece of joy' and indeed, Lo tse had a cute bouncy way of running about with her tail bouncing behind her that seemed to say: 'Oh! Life is a joy! Life is a joy! Life is a joy!' Ralphie Boy's posture and movements, on the other hand, seemed to be saying: 'Life is a bitch. Life is a bitch. Life is a bitch.'

The first thing each morning I would hear Lo tse scramble off her bed and go trotting down the passage towards the back door. 'Oh! Life is a joy! Life is a joy! Life is a joy!'

Ralphie Boy, curled up at the end of my bed, would narrowly open one eye, then the other, and look disapprovingly around the room. 'Oh, life is a bitch! Life is a bitch. Life is a bitch.' Ralphie Boy always timed things perfectly so he could have one good stretch before slinking off the bed and taking up his position on the side of the passage—about half-way along. As Lo tse came tumbling back through the back door, more bubbly than ever due to her state of post-first-crap-of-the-day satisfaction, Ralphie Boy would raise his paw.

Along the passage would come little Lo tse. Trot trot trot. Smile smile smile. 'Oh! Life is a joy! Life is a joy! Life is a joy!'

You couldn't say Ralphie Boy actually scratched Lo tse. It was more that Lo tse just ran along against his open claws.

'Oh, life is a joy! Life is a (*yelp!*) joy! Life is a joy!'

I don't know why Ralphie Boy was like he was. He'd had a normal secure kittenhood. I suppose if you have an inherently sour outlook on life it must be very annoying to see someone else—who has the exact same lot—very, very happy with it.

Yet I loved Ralphie. It's strange how we can love someone with few endearing or loving qualities. When he ran away my heart was quite broken for a while. However, I have since obtained a new cat —a gentle, tender and loving creature. And I think I love her more.

Jan Thorburn has published a number of books including a children's novel, Stranded*, set on a deserted New Zealand coastline. She lives in Auckland—dividing her time between writing, teaching English to new immigrants, and having quality time with her cat.*

Angel, Maybe

Heather McPherson

A letter to the *Listener* says that cats who eat birds clean up
incompetent members of the species.

I think about this.

My white cat's a hunter with yellow new-moon eyes.

She stalks birds.

I always thought the birds unlucky. Too slow, too young...

I've rescued, nursed and tenderly buried them.

But if they're incompetent?

And what if we generalise... to other species?

Last night I dreamt an enormous white cat

caught, played with, then ate my partner.

Tonight my partner undresses.

Her shoulderblades look like wings.

My white hair bristles, I stare yellow-eyed.

*Heather McPherson is a seventies lesbian feminist
who continues to eye the world with some
of the appalled wonder of the tribe and some of its
later modifications. She has published three books
of poems, has another in the pipeline and has
recently taken to prose with maybe a novel at
the end...*

A Cat's Best Friend

Dahlia Levy

They say a dog is man's best friend. If this is so, it must mean that a cat is woman's best friend. In the case of Kathryn Cott, she has served as the best friend to many stray cats over the years, providing them health, shelter and new homes.

'I have worked at Eastfield College, in Mesquite, Texas, for over eighteen years. I even graduated from there with two associate degrees. Over the years I have quietly tried to rescue and place kittens in good homes,' said Cott. 'In 1994, I rescued four kittens. Two were brought to me wet and cold, probably four to six weeks old and two I lured out of the main warren at the college with bits of chicken left over from my lunch.'

Out of those four kittens three died while Cott worked hard to nurse them back to health. 'I took them in for leukemia testing. They were both positive. Since they were already somewhat ill, I decided to put them to sleep,' said Cott. 'It broke my heart. The other one that died suffered from Coccidia and didn't like to take the medicine because it tasted bad back then.'

After that, Cott saw a period of time where she did not help many stray cats, but that all changed a few years later. 'In 1998, I was eating lunch outside when I observed a large black cat eating a cigarette butt. I gave him my leftover vegetables. I began bringing a small amount of food everyday after that,' said Cott. 'This cat and his buddies were living under the buildings in holes created by erosion from poor down-spout placement. One summer I noticed some of the cats had disappeared. I was told that they had been trapped and taken to the animal shelter. Most shelters are forced to destroy feral cats because they are not adoptable. I joined forces with a lady named Sami

Thompson to protest this. I did a lot of research on feral colonies and how to deal with them. I approached the current administration with a plan of trapping, neutering, administering shots, feeding, caring for and monitoring the cat population. I explained that TNR worked very well and reduced complaints. I had documentation to prove this and I gave this to the administration. I was told that a feral colony on our campus would violate the local leash law and make the college responsible for the cats if they bit someone.'

Since then, Cott has kept a record of every cat she has ever nursed and found a home for. It is a way to remember the first cats she helped, but was unable to save.

'It broke my heart. I grieved for months. I didn't even have a picture of them. I wanted a picture of them so-o-o bad,' said Cott about those first cats that passed away while in her care. 'While taking care of these cats I have made new friends, been stressed out and had a lot of fun. I even learned some things: feral behavior, new diseases, etc.' Cott has a record of every cat she has been able to help since 1999. Cott has gone from doing this by herself to actually forming an organisation to help the stray cats around the college were she works and other places as well.

Cott has done wonders for cats and she has even helped cat lovers realise the love they have for their own cats and the bond shared between them. I have found myself reminiscing about my cats and how our relationship developed. I used to hate cats. I came from a cat-hating family, so you can see where it came from, however that changed real quickly. My first year in college I dated a guy who had about ten cats/kittens. I would always walk over to his house since he didn't live too far away. I hated to admit it but they were so cute. Purring and hissing at each other. Always acting innocent. One day it hit me, I wanted one of them; okay, I wanted all of the kittens. I wanted to love them as much as they loved me when I went over there. I asked my father for a cat, but of course he said 'no'. However he surprised us by bringing home, for my mother, a cat who we all fell in love with. I lived on my own for a while and had a cat named Belle. She was my best friend. Recently I moved back home and both my mother's cat, Chyna and my cat live with us and we are one happy family. My family is now a cat/kitten-loving family, all because of Chyna and because of my first boyfriend. Women and cats will always seem to go hand-in-hand.

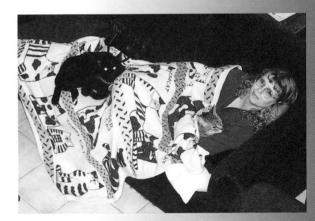

__Dahlia Levy__ is currently a student at Eastfield College where she is majoring in digital photography/imagery. The oldest child of Isaac and Sandi Levy, she was born in Dallas, Texas but was raised in Israel before returning back to the States. For more information please see
http://www.eastfieldcollege.com/ssi/spar/digital/cat/
or Kitico at www.kittico.org

Gestures

Beth Burrows

Mine is a life remarkably lacking in cats. The only cat around here at the moment is the orange one who regularly aggravates our dog by sunning herself on the grassy mound outside our door.

The only other cat I can recall is Mel Keegan's cat. But that was a long time ago. I had been warned that that cat was 'very unfriendly' and didn't like anyone. So I was surprised when the cat jumped into my lap, curled up, and started to purr. I was also surprised when Mel's husband started yelling at Mel to get that damned cat off of me and Mel started shouting at the cat to please leave me alone.

They kept on yelling and shouting, yelling and shouting, until the sound level became almost unbearable. At that point, the cat licked my hand, jumped off my lap, and went over and bit a leaf of the rubber tree that stood in the Keegan's living room.

It was then I noticed that there were a number of bite marks in the leaves.

Beth Burrows is president/director of the Edmonds Institute, a small public interest group in the US. Here is a picture of Beth Burrows taken in April, 2002, during an EarthWalk in Seattle in which Beth marched as a salmon. Beth is the fish on the left (of course).

k.d.—The Cat Who Knew Her Place
Margaret Young

I called her k.d. How else would I have someone of that name share my bed? She was small enough to stand on my outstretched hand. Meg, the vet's nurse, had rescued her from a hay-shed on a farm where her life was destined to be very short. We drove home with k.d prancing about on the passenger seat or tumbling off when I turned corners. She used those moments to explore under the seat or the brake pedal before being hastily plucked out of harm's way.

At home she quickly bonded to my slippers. She scampered about investigating rooms and corners till she realised she had lost me. When I answered her calls of distress she would bound back and stand expectantly in front of my slippers. It took her a while to realise there was a whole human being above them who provided food and cuddles and toys.

Because she was so tiny and had left her mother too early, I couldn't leave her alone all day, so she came to school with me. The empty guinea pig cage was hauled into the middle of the classroom and my 'special' students had a new stimulus in their day. k.d., however, was not satisfied spending her day looking through the wires of the cage. She soon learnt to clamber to the top where the wire mesh was bigger and squeeze through, much to the alarm of David who was afraid of small furry things, but liked to take off his shoes. A six-foot non-verbal teenager with a tiny kitten attached to the end of his sock was not his idea of fun.

With all the car travel and meeting excited children, k.d. became quite socialised and was not fazed by visitors to our house. In fact, visitors provided brief cases, back packs and plastic bags of things to be rummaged through and knees to climb on under the table while we ate or conducted our meetings. It was fun to watch the expressions on women's faces as k.d. jumped from one lap to the next. It was easy to tell who was a cat lover and who wasn't. Other cat-loving friends would include k.d. in their dinner invitations, and I was happy to take her along, till the time she got stuck behind the fridge! She set up such a yowling and spitting we feared my friend's adult cat was behind there with her... but he was in the next room looking just as alarmed as us. With superhuman effort I dragged the fridge aside and pulled out a spitting, scratching, writhing ball of rage and fear. Big drops of blood plopped onto the floor while I struggled to hold her still and locate the injury. Eventually I realised it was me who was bleeding from a seriously lacerated hand. k.d. did have a cut leg but no blood. I, on the other hand, required a patchwork of Band-aids before I was fit to take her to the vet where she stayed over night and had an almost severed tendon sewn up at great expense to me. When I collected her the vet said, 'No running and jumping for a while.'

Ha! The next day she jumped from the top of the stairs in pursuit of her toy mouse which she had playfully flicked through the banister.

This was just the beginning of k.d.'s mission to use up all of her nine lives as quickly as possible. Arriving home from work one day, I heard frantic meowing coming from the roof next door. I couldn't dissuade my eighty-six-year-old

neighbour from climbing his ladder on to the roof so I followed him up. k.d. was lost in the vast boxed-in spouting of two connected houses. All our clumping about only made her panic more and retreat further into the dark tunnels. I persuaded Mr R to come down and wait till she got hungry. Which she did and finally slunk into the kitchen wearing a veil of cobwebs and a seriously embarrassed expression.

Another time I found her tightly curled up on the couch soaking wet from head to tail. As I towelled her dry she purred vigorously while flicking her tail and casting fierce glances towards the back fence behind which lurked two swimming pools. Did she jump or was she pushed?

Late one night, after a long meeting, k.d. met me with an anxious look and her cute little white mouth rimmed in red. Her tongue was busy flicking in and out. I cradled her in my arms for a closer look. She had cut her tongue. It was tattered and frayed at the end. Where on earth had she been poking her nosey little nose this time? The vet was amazed. He said he doesn't normally sew up tongues but this one he had to… and trim off the frayed bits at the end. So, another extended stay at the vet's hospital. When I paid her a visit she showed her appreciation by staggering up on her groggy legs and hissing at me. Back at home she carried on as usual, washing herself and eating crunchy food despite the stitches in her tongue and the vet's advice.

So k.d. continues to bound through life not wasting an opportunity to have an adventure. She has a chunk out of one ear and has occasionally lost bits of fur defending her back yard. She is often inadvertently shut in cupboards, down the back of drawers, the clothes dryer, the garden shed because she is too busy poking about to notice I have shut her in. She just waits patiently till I find her after a frantic search and much calling on my part.

When I come home, before I reverse down the drive, I usually put her in the car with me. She likes to play chicken. I prefer to have her sitting on the dashboard where I can see her. Sometimes, I don't catch her and, when I stop, I find her in the carport lying behind the back wheel with her legs playfully in the air.

To compensate for these cheeky acts, k.d. brings me presents. In her kitten days she brought me twigs and real birds and mice left under the furniture for me to sniff out later. One bird she put in a cupboard overnight and retrieved it next morning still alive. Now, in her slightly more sensible age, she brings me her toy mouse, calling through clenched lips and dropping it at my feet. What greater gift could I wish for?

So, I forgive her for sleeping in all the forbidden places… under the doona in the guest room, on couches, in the basket of clean washing and the kitchen sink after I have let the water out. But her favourite place is as I had anticipated… my bed. Sorry, that other k.d., you have missed your chance!

Margaret Young is a special education teacher. She loves her work but prefers to be a circus performer with POW Circus. Aerials and stilt-walking are her favourite skills. She loves to travel and ride her mountain bike whenever she gets the chance. Her grown-up twin daughters have ceased to be surprised at what their mother does next.

Yoshi

Janine Le Couteur

A lizard on its back
dead
with silver hard belly
tail sliced, two legs gone
how many more creatures maimed or killed
sleeps inside, but still he is instinct
poised to catch movement.

The urge to find him was strong
from despair and loss, instinct also led me
on the sixth visit we only half noticed him, son and I
cage on top, second to the right
small handful of soft, strong purr
vibrating, resounding from somewhere deep
comforting, balming, nestling animal
encouraged my heart to soften
lotus opening.

We welcomed him
immediately after he chose us
we are his more than he is ours
though sometimes he is of us
then cries for solitude and night time prowls
when doors are closed.

Strong, elegant, handsome cat
playful friend takes his aim
wraps and slaps his front legs around ours
spontaneity exposed in all its joy
too busy chatting on the phone
animal reaches quietly up and gently bites
ahh! yes breakfast... I had forgotten.

And madness when the breeze strengthens
stalks leaves and swaying grasses
throws his toy into my lap
skitterish cat races down the hallway
skids on rugs on polished floors
jumps at anything.

Vaccum and washing machine terrify him.

Never quite owned nor quite domesticated
always himself
part cat, part human, part ancient feline spirit
his pale green eyes, the daily absence
solitude and languishing stretches
his smooches and graceful indulgence
always dead giveaways.

Lovely puss
instinct poised once again.

Janine Le Couteur *has been*
writing on and off for many
years. Her writing is an
expression of her outer and
inner world experiences.
Janine shares her life with her
son Gabriel, Yoshi their cat
and her friends.

Cat Burglar

Jill Wilson

I'd never broken into anyone's house before but it was dark and cold so I figured that most people would be inside on a Saturday night. My friend Jill held the ladder while I climbed over the fence dividing the front and back yard. The headlights of a passing car caught me, leg slung over the top, about to drop into back of the property. No reaction from the driver. Are burglaries now de rigueur in Footscray? I proceed towards the back door. Locked. Predictably. What to do?

Inside the house a muffled sound. I need to break in! The back section of the house is a lean-to bathroom and laundry fitted with… yes… louvres. I'm in business. I edge each slice of glass out of the slat. It's easy; someone has done this before. Then tumble through the window into the laundry trough. More sounds, a faint yowling. 'I'm coming Eddie!' Into the kitchen, a door between me and my missing cat. 'I'm coming!' Cat noises increase in velocity. Hand on the doorknob, a twist. Locked. From the other side. Cat stranded on one side, me on the other.

In the front garden I confer with Jill. Eddie, the nuggety black manx who lives with me has been missing for twenty-four hours. A plaintive yowl emanates from under the front door of the Victorian weatherboard across the road. Eddie is trapped. Sociable, party animal, Eddie is trapped in Sven and Angela's house. Number 8. A place he considers his own. Part of his street. The mayor of the street he is. Un-elected, sure but as certain in his role as your old-style, working-class, Labor-voting number-cruncher on Footscray Council. Eddie has visitation rights in a few houses in Stirling Street, dogs or not. An open door is an invitation. And he's very fond of this open door. He loved Muriel who lived at number 8 or close by for most of her eighty years. Had his own mohair blanket when Muriel was living there. Now Sven and Angela rent the house. They like cats and Eddie has adjusted to the newly sanded floorboards and the techno.

'Arwwwlllll'. The hungry, distressed yowl. It's Saturday night of a long weekend. How long will my neighbours be away? I re-climb the fence, squirm through the window and check the contents of their fridge. Very clean, very spartan. They're away until Monday night. What to do?

There's a decent space under the door which blocks Eddie from an easy exit. Where the carpet was ripped up to expose the boards. I can slip my fingers underneath and he bends down and noses my hand. 'Arwwwlllll'. Some food is possible. I re-trace my steps home and get dry food. Climb, drop, shimmy through window, shove crunchies through the gap. 'Arwwwlllll'.

I made the ladder-louvre journey three more times before Sven and Angela returned to release Eddie to his fiefdom of the street. They were grateful there was no longer carpet in the house; I was glad my break-and-enter career was over.

Three years on, Eddie has white hairs amongst the black fur and a saggy belly. Random visits through open doors are still part of his repertoire. Like some old blokes, he struggles with incontinence and may be a less desirable visitor nowadays. But we have been together for thirteen years and he still wants to snuggle up on cold nights. What to do? Repeated visits to the vet.

Treated with a female hormone more commonly used for female dogs, he takes the tablets placidly but no improvement in his condition. I return to the vet after weeks of treatment. A new vet surveys the situation. 'That's a strange treatment to try on him. Did you notice anything unusual while he was on the medication?' 'He was in a lot of cat fights. There were stray cats hanging around every night. In fact I've had a new front fence built to keep them out.' The vet laughs. Poor Eddie's been exuding female hormones for weeks, been the obscure object of desire for toms for miles around. Been both puzzled and incontinent, harassed and under siege.

My old mate sleeps outside now and it's hard to ignore his cry at the door on cold nights. 'Arwwwlllll.' 'Let me in.' During the day he holds court in the street, balancing on the new picket fence or lying in the middle of the road forcing vehicles to stop. Cat burglar, street brawler, mayor and presser of Stirling Street flesh, the street, and my life, will be the poorer when he goes.

 *As children, **Jill Wilson** and her sisters tamed stray cats and sneaked them into their bedroom after dark so their pet-despising father would not know. As soon as she had her own house, she acquired a cat. Eddie, Jing and Alley are the three cats who currently live with her.* 🐾

The Feral Cats

Coral Hull

As our guilt over the destruction of Australia's ecosystems grows ever greater, we look around for someone else to blame, which is usually in the form of someone who has not got the voice to defend themselves. In this case, it is the cat who has gone wild (the feral cat), either escaped or lost into the bush. We kill the feral cat and in this way we hope to kill our own guilt. The scape-goating of bush cats in Australia has added yet more to this country's hard and mean personality that we have tried so hard to hide with Ockerisms. Inland mateship has always been two drunken 'Aussies' hanging a dead cat in a tree outside William's Creek in South Australia. Animals are slaughtered (murdered) because they are property (with no legal rights) and also slaughtered because they are not as yet property, such as in the case of bush cats. There are many justifications for cruelty and murder and genocide. We need to justify something when we know that it is morally wrong. When we judge anything outside ourselves, people and cats included, we are really turning to face our own judge in the mirror that the world has become. It is our own actions that will finally condem us and not those of the cat. The world mirror reflects who we are as individuals and as a species. We can only ever hope to catch a glimpse of understanding of the amazing animal that is: The Cat.

the feral cats are clearing the forests for dairy
farming/ they are sticking their sharp claws into
the soil/ they are ploughing it/ straight through
the heart of our dusty continent/ in the kimberleys
the bungle bungles/ in kakadu/ the feral cats eat
yellow cake too/ they are capitalists/ drug pushers/
& if they ever knew the value of amazon burgers/
we'd have dangerous competitors/

                    the feral cats are
into destruction/ taking advantage of endangered
civilisations/ the wildlife not trained to defend
themselves/ against super speed/ sharp claws &
teeth/ they massacred the koories/ when they came
to this country/ they ripped out the forests in
preference to beef/

                    the n.p.w.s. really expose them
for what they are/ feral cats have even migrated to
tasmania/ they are destroying rivers/ & are lighting
bushfires/ the lemonthyme/ douglas aspley/ huon
valley & denison spires/ they are tearing down
mountains/ with blood stained claws/ they turn
coastline wilderness/ into tourist resorts/ with
their massive jaws/

                    arsonists/ murderers/ rapists
& thieves/ the damage they do/ to fragile planet
ecology/ has to be seen/ to be believed/ & not only
that/ they are erecting buildings/ in the remaining
greenery/ they are/ kidnapping children/ & are
bashing their wives/ society was peaceful/ until
they arrived/

                    you better believe it/ they're
destroying the scenery/ i think we should bring in
the military/ they are an imminent danger to
civilisation/ an ecological threat/ if we bait the
trees with pesticides/ & drown their kittens in
sewerage pipes/ & burn down their habitat/ & drop
the bomb/ we'll beat them yet/ & if that doesn't work
we're in trouble

Coral Hull is the author of over
thirty-five books of poetry, fiction,
artwork and digital photography.
Coral is the editor and publisher of
Thylazine, *an electronic journal
featuring articles, interviews,
photographs and the recent work of
Australian writers and artists. She
lives in Darwin, in the Northern
Territory, Australia with her two dog
companions Binda and Kindi.*

n.p.w.s. = national parks & wildlife service

The End of the Cat Door

Dawn Osborne

When Neesha and Asha, our Burmese 'girls', joined our household they gained that coveted privilege of having the run of the house and being able to come and go as they pleased. Within reason, that is. I was adamant that we should know if they were 'in' or 'out' so a cat flap was out of the question at the start. However, after a couple of years of getting up and down to them several times in an evening, it was decided that there was definitely some merit in a cat door that would allow them to come and go freely.

A suitable door was installed and some serious coaching took place to get them to use it. 'Use food rewards,' we were told but why would two over-indulged cats be interested in contorting their heads and bodies through a perspex flap to receive a bit of dried food that's readily available anyway.

In desperation with our 'not very bright' feline friends, one Saturday we decided to give them the idea by fixing the flap fully open. It worked like a dream and all day long they happily trotted in and out and I didn't seem to mind not knowing if they were in or out.

As evening fell we debated whether to close the flap. Since it was Saturday our favourite TV programme 'The Bill' was scheduled. Wouldn't it be great to watch it without being disturbed by little faces at the window, appealing to be let in? It was a pleasant balmy night and, since the girls had acted so responsibly all day, the decision was made to leave the flap open.

Now Neesha and Asha are two very different cats even though they are half sisters. Asha is like the kitten that never grew up; lilac and cream she loves to be around her mama, be the subject of lots of cuddles, attention and 'cat chat'. Neesha, a pretty lithe 'blue', is a true outdoors girl, full of adventurous spirit.

Whereas Asha would be lucky to catch a moth with a broken wing, Neesha rarely misses the prey she stalks despite sporting bells and other paraphernalia around her neck. The greatest 'prize' Asha ever presented us with was half a hard-boiled egg discarded in the garden from a workman's lunch. But the feathers of Neesha's unfortunate victims have been known to adorn our verandah.

When the idea of having cats was first mooted, my husband had some reservations and was quick to point out the drawbacks—we won't be able to go away, they might have fleas and, for someone who dislikes being close to birds and small mammals, they bring in all sorts of little creatures. I reassured him on all these points and particularly the last, 'They won't bring in little creatures because we won't let them.'

Saturday night, best night of the week with home-made pizzas, a good wine and, at 8.30p.m., 'The Bill'. We were happily installed in the best seats in the house and the girls were trotting in and out with a great sense of independence. Settling ourselves in, we were content in this new regime that meant we could indulge our Saturday night passion without interruption at the window or door.

The dramatic tension was not especially high on the screen but our favourite police characters moved through the plot. Suddenly, from the corner of my eye, I spotted Neesha some way across the floor. She was standing erect and proud, looking deliberately in my direction. From where I was seated, she looked as if she had sprouted a big long mandarin-style moustache.

'Oh, there's Neesha,' I said, 'She looks as if she's got something in her mouth.'

My husband's chair was significantly closer to Neesha and I'd have to say that I've never seem him (or a person of his sizeable frame) move so fast.

'It's a fucking rat,' he exclaimed and shot up as if someone had pressed an ejector button!

I smelt panic in the air and, as repulsed as I was by the idea of a rat let loose in the house, I knew someone had to take control.

Assuming a brave façade and using calming gestures, I announced, 'Leave this to me. Just don't panic.' Inside, fully aquiver, I was thinking, 'What now?' I dashed to

the cupboard under the kitchen sink and grabbed the fly swat—what on earth I hoped to achieve with that I don't know.

By this time, Neesha had darted into the front room and was ready for action and a bit of fun, crouching beside an armchair, rat still in her grip. Neesha loves to play 'hide and seek' when I chase her around the house and she dives for cover behind a chair or the drapes, leaving just the tip of her tail or hint of a paw for me to seek her out. But this was no game as I tried to get across to her with my firm but useless tones.

Still unsure whether the rat was dead or alive, I rushed to slam shut the doors in the room—at least if I had to chase a live rat it would be confined.   What could I say? Certainly not, 'Neesha drop it.' I knew the damn thing was more than my fly swat could handle.

'Stay there,' I commanded and luckily this is a phrase our girls understand. I stealthily crept from the room having decided upon a more rational approach. This tactic needed more sophisticated equipment and so this time I armed myself with a stiff hand brush and an empty shoe box.

Guardedly, I re-entered the lounge and, to my horror, saw Neesha sitting on her haunches with bright expectant eyes fixed on me but minus one big, dark rodent moustache. 'The rat is on the loose,' I gasped to myself (husband having taken cover long since). Ever so quietly, I crept from chair to chair, peering around the back and sides but with no help from my Burmese friend who thought this was great sport. She followed my every move with her huge amber eyes, determined not to give the game away.

Closing in on the chair in the corner I clambered onto the seat and looked over the back. There it was! An enormous great rat, lying on its side—but was it dead? I knew the fly swat would come in handy and tentatively, ever so tentatively, I prodded the beast and learnt with relief that Neesha had done her job cleanly and thoroughly. It's interesting how fear changes our perceptions—no longer afraid of this creature I realised how very beautiful it was, from its cute little face to its silky grey coat.

Using the brush I flipped the deceased into the shoe box and ceremoniously carried it to the bottom of the garden for a fitting burial among the tall pines that flank the compost bins. Neesha wanted to be part of the funeral cortege and by this stage Asha was on the scene too. But a few moments of solitary calm were needed to restore my equilibrium and so the girls were made to stay indoors.

As for the cat flap, it had a very short life. Anyway, whether through dull intellect or a desire to be waited on, our cats seemed fairly determined not to use it properly. So, we are back to playing doorkeeper but at least we can screen the associates our girls bring home.

Dawn Osborne was born in the UK and grew up with four brothers and two sisters plus a whole menagerie of cats, dogs, birds and reptiles. She came to Australia in 1983 and had a very busy and intense career in secondary teaching which left no time to have animals. In 1999 she decided upon a career change into real estate; it was time at last to get back to having some animals around. Thus Neesha and Asha, two Burmese females, joined their household and are very much part of their family.

Attacked Cat—9/11/01

Ellen Redding Kaler

A survivor
of the bombings
made the news
three weeks after
the attacks.

A cat is found—
ghostly looking,
powdered by debris
and fall out—
wild looking,
made feral by
panic in the
apocalypse.

Yet he wore tags,
ID, so his vet
could be called,
his owners traced.

Nobody's home.

Home was too close
to ground zero.

The orphaned cat
is celebrated—
another innocent victim—
another perspective on loss,
survival and recovery.
This cat is heroic
because he's forgiven
his owner's absence.
He's not planning
revenge with claws or
counter bombings with
hairballs, just
plotting how now to live,
be fed, grow strong,
getting comfort
by giving comfort.

We all want to hold him—
to coax back his purr—
to adopt and protect him,
to say, 'It will be all right,'
though life will never
be the same.

Ellen Redding Kaler *enjoys a long history with cats: from Tommy J. Junior who used to attack her in her Mickey Mouse pyjamas, through Ears who starred on stage in 'I Remember Mama' with her in high school, to Gaston, Gus, Griselda, and Gabriel who came to live with her during her first teaching job, to Bart-hollow-mew and Jacob who graced FarmSong, to the housecat in current residency: Mellow.*

And So Do Cats

Lyn McConchie

'Terrorists!' said the chap buying one of my coloured lambs. 'Bastards are everywhere lately.' 'So are cats,' I said, observing Fluffy my barn-cat as she drifted by.

I returned to the house to find the inside-cats, Tiger and Dancer, jockeying for position at the food bowl. Since Fluff currently has two kittens at the scampering stage in the hay barn, the illusion that everywhere I walk, there is a cat underfoot, is being remarkably well sustained at the moment.

'Terrorists!' a friend commented, some days later, 'They sneak in when no one's looking.' 'So do cats,' I muttered, recalling the previous evening. I'd been sitting in bed, legs stretched out, back propped against pillows, reading an engrossing book as I ate dinner one-handed. Somewhere in there, I'd woken up to the fact I seemed to have less dinner than I recalled eating. I paused to ponder this. At which time, a small regular noise manifested itself. I peered over the edge of the bed. There was Tiger, happily ensconced on the carpet, gnawing his way though one of the two pieces of grilled fish with which I'd started my meal.

Like terrorists too, sometimes my cats just aren't so unobtrusive. Fluffy marches into the kitchen at any time I leave both porch doors open, however briefly. Once there, she leaps on Tiger's and Dancer's feed bowls, empties them in great gulps, looks around quickly, sees nothing more edible, and demands the door be opened at once so she may depart again. What am I, a prison warder? Don't I know she has kittens to attend. Meekly I open the door. It's probable some terrorists force on their victims that same feeling of helpless cooperation.

Cats infiltrate in other ways too. Tiger starts by curling up at the end of my bed. As I sink deeper into my book after dinner, he shifts. I never see him move but somehow when, after an hour or two of steady reading, I come back to myself, it's invariably to find that fourteen pounds of spotted Ocicat has oozed his way in and is curled up, apparently asleep, in my lap. He isn't asleep, of course. If I query his presence he's always awake enough to look up innocently and claim invitation. My lap was empty, wasn't it?

'Terrorists!' snarled my mate next door. 'From the media reports it sounds as if we're all in bed with them and don't know it.' 'Same as cats,' I note. Well, it is with Tiger in particular. Although I do usually find out about that eventually. Cold nights annoy him. He dawdles into the bedroom, leaps lightly onto the

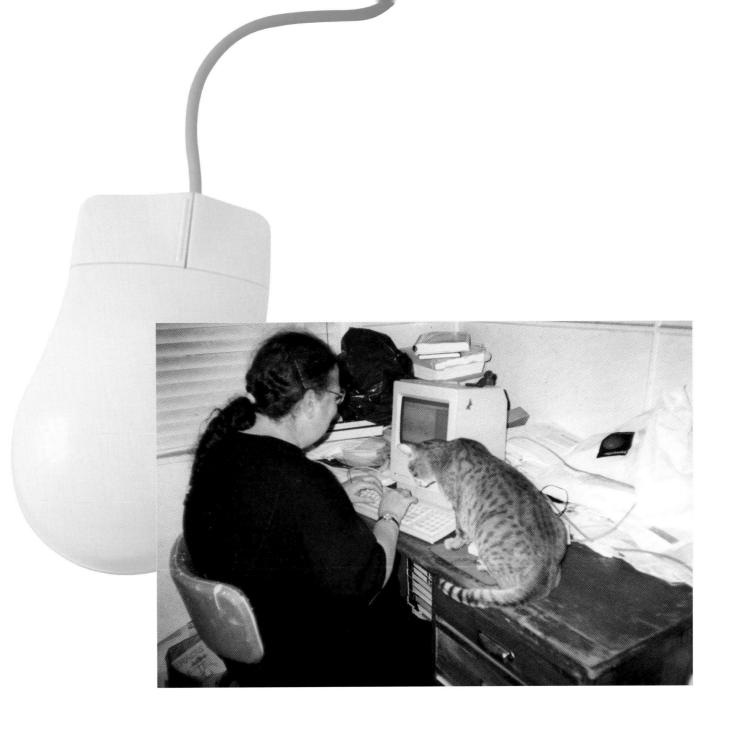

end of the bed and slinks to where the bedclothes are wrapped around my shoulders. Unobtrusively he hooks them loose. Then he slides between a couple of blankets, moves down to hip-level, and snuggles in. If he does it well I won't wake, and he's in the warm until morning—which is a little too late for eviction purposes.

'Terrorists!' someone said in the library when I was there last week. 'They try to make us believe their way, *and* they think we're all stupid.' 'Same as cats,' I say to my armload of library books. Cats think humans exist to keep them warmed, fed, cuddled, and loved. Humans exist to open doors, cat-food tins, and cartons large enough for a cat to curl up in. Our opinion, that cats exist to keep us company, doesn't begin to describe the relationship of a cat and their human.

Humans are stupid too, in the estimation of the same average cat. No tail, no whiskers—no brains. Certainly our language abilities in feline-speak are incredibly limited. We come in useful for some things but, it can take so long to get the essential demand across, I think Tiger assumes I'm something of a moron.

'What the anti-terrorist squads need is the sort of training which teaches them to identify targets on sight,' complained a lady of my acquaintance. 'I came back on the plane from Brisbane recently and they held me up over a bottle-opener in my handbag. What did they think I was going to do with *that*?'

Since the lady in question is fifty-six and half-crippled with arthritis, I saw her point. She could also be right. People in that line of work do need a terrorist to study. Someone to watch, learn all their tricks and, maybe, master the ability to pick exactly the right moment to pounce. So I'd suggest, instead of human tutors, the anti-terrorist squads of various countries should take lessons from cats. Anyone who learns well enough to out-smart a cat could easily beat a terrorist. And besides—Fluffy has kittens. I'm looking for good homes.

Lyn McConchie is a New Zealand writer who began writing professionally in 1991. To date she has sold fourteen books—six in America, and over 175 short stories spread around many countries. She shares her nineteenth century farmhouse with two cats and seven thousand books.

Fussl: A Very Special Cat

Sandra Schürle

It all begun in 1989. I was thirteen years old.

My father decided that my mother would get a very special Christmas present —a cat. Although I hadn't been in the least excited about this idea, I had to admit that the cat we collected from the Animal Shelter, called Fussl, was beautiful. He was two years old, had a whitish belly and face with a brown dot on his nose. It was this dot that gave him a certain *je-ne-sais-quoi* and made him special even just to look at. My father had fallen in love with him instantly.

But Fussl's initiation into our family proved difficult, to put it mildly. He bit, scratched, hissed and behaved altogether more like a feral beast than the sweet pussy cat we had imagined would join our family. We could not go near him without heavy padded gardening gloves. Forget stroking, playing, least of all cuddling! The animal shelter gave us many hints but the weeks passed without any improvement. Although we found all of this rather difficult we grew increasingly fond of Fussl. He was the first port of call when we came home and the last to say good night to. Not a day passed without the whole family agonising over how to turn Fussl into a 'normal' cat.

We decided that he might perhaps be happier as an outdoor cat. All went well initially: he marched around in the garden thoroughly inspecting everything. And for the first time he looked peaceful and contented. We were very happy, hoping change was in the air. Until the day when he did not return from his garden walk. Nor did he turn up the next day or the next after that. We were all terribly worried and had horrible thoughts about what might have happened to him. And we missed him intensely, day in, day out. His disappearence had left a big gap. Although he had been so elusive and difficult, Fussl had become an integral part of us in a very short time. The worst was not knowing, not getting answers to why he had behaved in this way, where he had gone, what had become of him. But maybe it was precisely these unanswered questions that made us continue day after day to look for him.

This time of great sorrow and worry made my family become very close. I discovered a sensitve and raw side to both my parents and my sister that I never before even knew existed.

The desire for Fussl to return was the one side of the coin, the longing for an animal companion the other. We thought that our sadness might be tempered if we had another cat in the house. And so July joined us. A brown tabby with big round eyes and huge pussy paws, she was only ten weeks old. July was clearly no Fussl replacement: apart from the age difference, they had totally different characters. Even after we had very happily accepted that July had joined us for good, we never really gave up looking for Fussl.

As fate would have it, one day Fussl stood at our door. We couldn't trust our eyes or believe our luck. It wasn't just me who cried that evening! Finally good fortune was on our side: it was also love at first sight between Fussl and July after their initial round of sniffing. Just as well: it does not bear thinking what would have happened otherwise as from this day we were

determined to not be without either of these two cats.

Fussl—and July as well—became important markers of the rest of my childhood. They consoled me when I sobbed unbearably during my first heartbreak; they saw me leave home—and return. Unbelievably, Fussl had returned from his 'excursion' a changed soul: tame, sweet as pie and totally devoted to us. He trailed us wherever we went and the pinnacle of his bliss was to rub his head against our forehead. There was not a day when he didn't tell us how thankful and happy he was to be with us again. And lying belly up he never fogot to remind us of our stroking duties and lovingly put his paw on our laps.

Both cats contributed majorly to my harmonious and happy childhood and I remain incredibly grateful to them. Even today when I think 'family', they are automatically part of my thoughts. Sadly on the first of July in 2002, because of old age, we had to put Fussl to sleep. This time saying goodbye was real and for ever. Again our family became very close. Together we cried and grieved and talked endlessly about Fussl's long life and the quirky events of his—and our—past. We had lost an important family member and a dear friend. July remains with us, is happy and healthy, and gives us lots of peasure. But we already knew that Fussl was irreplaceable and so his place in our hearts and lives remain special and forever his.

Sandra Schürle *was born in August 1976 in a small citiy near Vienna. Her father's work took her parents to Vienna for two years. In 1977 they moved to Hoefingen, a very small village about eighteen kilometres away from Stuttgart, where both her parents grew up. She spent her childhoood in beautiful contryside. Today she lives in Schwieberdingen, close to her parents. She works as an International Account Manager in a company doing direct marketing.*

Paris…

Sheryl Topperwien

Orange, like marmalade... light-and-dark, ginger-striped, piercing green Egyptian eyes; she was a striking cat. But she was certainly no aristocrat. I rescued her, as a small kitten, from a restaurant carpark—she was one of a family of strays residing there.

I was concerned that this sweet little cat, sunning herself in the early morning sun, would fall victim to one of the many car wheels she was living among. So I took her to the local vet to see if a better-located home could be found. Surprisingly, it was easy to approach this kitten. Other feral kittens I had seen in the carpark always scattered when approached, but this one stood its ground and meowed as if to complain, perhaps just because she could.

I had four dogs, so I didn't think that taking the kitten home would be a wise move. On examination, the vet informed me that the kitten had cat flu and needed treatment before they could try to find her a home. I agreed to phone in a couple of weeks, just to keep track of her progress. Before I left, I had a departing chat with my new, small friend and I wished her good luck and a safe journey in life. She replied by purring loudly and cuddling into my neck most affectionately and I felt the beginning of the special bond that was destined to grow between us.

Two weeks passed and I called the vet to enquire. The news was that the kitten, though growing strong, still had cat flu and, because of this, no home could be found. The vet agreed to continue trying to place her in a good home, but added that unless a home could be found soon, the kitten would need to be euthanased.

That first loud thank-you purr and nuzzling at my neck had created a bond that made it impossible for me to leave her stranded; I needed to come to her rescue once again.

The cat, whom I named Paris, settled in well with the four dogs already in residence, particularly with an eight-month-old, lively kelpie cross. They seemed to like the same games. The dogs were all comfortable with a cat about the place—I'd had one or two over the years—and, although the older dogs paid her no attention, generally, harmony was maintained.

The name Paris seemed to suit her, even though she had very ordinary blood-lines. She had attitude and spirit, and a certain stately nature... She didn't seem like a Fluffy or a Sooty; something bigger and bolder suited her personality. Her true nature began to shine, right from the start, playing fearlessly with the young dog, scampering up and down screen doors and curtains and demanding food often, by meowing loud and long, and she soon became a prominent member of the household. It was her bold yet cuddly demeanour that won the hearts of friends who came and neighbours whose houses she frequented.

Paris had a way of making her presence felt. If she wanted you to open a screen door for her entry or departure, she would take a flying leap at the door, scrambling up and then thudding down on the hard timber floor, not once but repeatedly, until her bidding was done.

One day a neighbour phoned to tell me that, if I was looking for my cat, she could be found socialising at a party the neighbour was hosting. Apparently Paris was soaking up the attention offered to her by the guests. Paris also regularly made herself at home on the end of this woman's bed, sometimes staying away for a day or two at a time.

Another neighbour informed me, while chatting over the front fence, that a couple of days earlier she had enlisted the postman's help to escort her and her dog past a hazard on the road. On further enquiry, it turned out that the hazard had been Paris, teasing a small brown snake—in the middle of the road. I wasn't sure whether I should

have been concerned that Paris was playing on the road, or that the object of her attention was dangerous or that she was interrupting the smooth running of the neighbourhood by holding up residents. I smiled, and the conversation moved on.

Paris visited several households in close proximity to our home, claiming and being granted tenancy at each one. Paris was probably so wild and free spirited because of her early feral beginnings. Her naturally affectionate nature, and kinship with people and other animals, would have been enhanced by the weeks spent at the vet's, at a young age, being hand-fed and having human companionship and her bold and outgoing nature was able to develop by sharing a house with four dogs who accepted and played with her.

Paris was a challenge of a cat, a unique blend of her own heritage and her environment, and it was a hard decision to leave her behind when I moved house last year. I saw that Paris was attached to the land and to her community and its people, not just to me— a result of her freelancing feral temperament and bold social nature.

I decided that she would probably be happiest in the environment she had created for herself, and there was no shortage of offers to give her a permanent home at neighbouring houses. Regular reports indicate that Paris is alive and thriving... a truly individual cat.

Sheryl Topperwien is forty-six, and about to commence a degree course in social science, majoring in gender studies which she finds extremely exciting. Previously she has been, in the main, self employed, having dabbled in real estate, been manager and proprietor of a large and busy licensed restaurant, and run a secretarial service, among other things. She adores animals and, as an adult especially, has always had several cats and dogs in her life at any one time. 🐾

Section Four CATalysts

Gryphon

Evelyn Moseley

Having the responsibility of caring and looking after an animal is something very special. It creates a unique bond that results in a two way relationship. I have that type of bond with Gryphon, and I am happy to say it will only get stronger in the years to come.

Gryphon came to my home when she was just two months old. I was scared because she was so tiny, a real little fluff ball. She is an Exotic Shorthair, a mixture of Persian and British Shorthair. She has a pug nose and wide face, a thick tortoise shell coat and big coppery gold eyes. She's just beautiful. I placed an order for her with a breeder before she was born and I eagerly awaited her arrival. I had done some research beforehand about the different types of cat breeds and found she was right one for me. Everything was prepared: her litter tray, her plates and bowl, even her scratching pole. I tried to cater to all her needs. It was December and the Christmas tree was up and decorated. Its glitter and sparkle amused her for hours on end. I think it was on that first day that we established a bond.

As I have a physical disability and I use an electric wheelchair to get around, Gryphon quickly caught on that my lap is always available to her if she wants a nap. Nowadays she recognises the sound of my chair moving. She knows my movements. She knows that when I move away from the table or my computer desk, my lap is hers. She knows that she can always use my chair as a stepping stone. If I can come to her aid, I will. She often climbs onto the headrest of my wheelchair and will be content sitting and looking down at everyone and everything. She is also aware that if she is on my lap or headrest she will go for a ride and has to balance herself. I used to worry about the wheels of my chair running over her paws or her tail but she obviously trusts me. She often gets behind the wheelchair (when I'm in it) and hides.

She seems to be aware of my disability and the fact that I can't hold her or pat her like other people can. It makes me wonder if that's the reason why she will sit only on my lap and nobody else's. Is it because I can't move and disturb her? Or is it because she feels safe with me? I prefer to think it's because she feels safe. Whenever she is around me she is so patient and she keeps a check on where I am, just like I keep a check on where she is. If she goes outside she comes back in every so often to see where I am and who I'm with.

I can't help but feel proud when I see her outside pouncing on butterflies in the garden. She is so agile and quick. She always brings her catch inside to show me. I am lucky she isn't a climber so she doesn't catch birds.

For years I dreamed about owning a cat. To me, Gryphon is a joy to have around. I am always laughing at her antics and she has filled me with a sense of belonging. She has become another part of myself and I would be completely lost without her. That saying I once heard is true…
'Happiness is being owned by a cat'!

Evelyn Moseley is in her forties and is currently studying welfare studies. She lives in a unit with Gryphon. Evelyn is a Cancerian and like all Cancerians she loves staying home; with Gryphon, of course!

The Boys

Lesley Higgs and Jenny Kelly

These stories tell how two little boys made their way into our hearts and forever changed our lives.

Lesley's story

Our boys were born in a haystack on a vineyard in Moriac, Victoria and, for some unknown reason, their mum took off for greener pastures when they were about four weeks old. Jenny and I had been thinking about a pet for a while and had been mulling over the idea of a labrador or cocker spaniel. But we were a bit unsure about the amount and smell of doggie presents in the backyard and, after all, just who would clean it up?

We had recently cat-minded a beautiful, old, female cat for friends and been introduced to our new neighbours' gorgeous tortoiseshell, so when we heard about the abandoned kittens in the haystack, we decided that having a look might be an idea. We found three tiny, tabby kittens at the vineyard. One especially took my heart because it was the smallest and most timid. And it was beautifully coloured. This little one, although starving, was too scared to come out from under the tractor to accept the offered food. I ended up under the tractor in an attempt to reassure it and left some food before crawling back out. From this moment, I was a goner as far as being a prospective kitten mother goes.

Jenny and I discussed the pros and cons of cat adoption over the next couple of days and eventually set out to rescue the three kittens. We decided if we could catch them, we'd take them to the vet to be cleaned up and immunised. We would keep the smallest female and we were confident that the vet would find homes for the other two. However, we managed to rescue only two kittens, after pulling a sizable wood-pile apart twice before we discovered them in their tunnel system under the last piece of wood. After securing the two hissing, spitting, snarling and very annoyed feral kittens in a cage, we set out to visit the vet, comfortable in the knowledge that our little female pussycat would soon be sitting quietly on our laps and purring, enjoying our love and affection.

The vet scene is one I will remember forever. My radical feminist partner always said that if she had ever had children it would be her karma to have twin boys. This premonition was about to come true! I thought the vet was very brave as he politely nodded his acknowledgement to me when I told him to be very careful of the vicious kittens. He reached in for the first 'patient', examined Number One kitten—and proclaimed it a boy. Jenny smiled and informed me that this was the one to let go to another home. The vet then bravely reached in for Number Two, the beautiful, smaller cat and announced that it too was a boy. Jen's eyes widened and her jaw dropped as she stood there in stunned silence before asking the vet if he were really sure. The vet assured her politely that he had indeed examined many kittens in his time and was very definitely sure. What to do: it looked like we had just become mothers to twin boys!

This is how our boys, named Mori (born in Moriac) and Woody (found in a woodpile) became part of our family from that point on. We both left the clinic with tears in our eyes, mine from laughing and Jenny's from trying to come to terms with the inevitability of her karma.

Jenny's postscript

Who would have thought that two tiny kittens—and boys at that—could bring so much love, joy and laughter into a household? I grew up on a farm where I was taught animals were there to work, certainly not to be just loved and pampered. That's all very well but in the short time Mori and Woody have been part of our lives, they have taught me lots of other things: how to pander to their every wish, how to smile endlessly about their little games and how to perfect tummy rubs. Each cat has his own unique 'cat-onality', and both are full of 'cat-itude'! Mori is the affectionate one and, if I have been working for too long on the computer, he will come and jump on my lap and demand full attention and a tummy rub. In the past I would have continued to work and remain oblivious to the outside world. Nowadays, thanks to Mori, I take regular breaks, smile and laugh a lot, play silly games—and find the quality of my work improved!

I have also learnt that you cannot make a cat do anything! Woody, originally the smaller and shyer of the two, is now quite big and the true boss of the family. Woody will do exactly what he wants and when he wants it! And we just smile. Pandering to the boys and letting them get away with just about anything—now that's not something I had imagined I'd ever do!

Cats are wonderful animals. As long as we love them, feed them and give them lots of cuddles and tummy rubs they seem content. Their own personal 'outdoor park'—the deluxe model!—has also met with great approval (and lets the birds survive as well).

Mori and Woody have been part of our family for only two-and-a-half years. I often wonder how I lived so long without knowing the love and joy that cats bring.

Lesley Higgs is a psychiatric nurse and studies health promotion and horticulture. She admits to not being a cat person—that is, until Mori and Woody became part of the family.

Jenny Kelly shares her life by the sea with Lesley, four goldfish and two cats. She has just finished her PhD on lesbians and menopause. She is a registered midwife and a sessional tutor at Deakin University.

Cats Leaving Paw Prints on My Heart

Liselotte Lässig

When I was nearly five, I was struck with polio. My left leg remained lame and I had to wear an ugly, painful, hated iron thing. I couldn't run like the other kids; I wasn't as fast as them, but I tried to keep up. With my good leg, I could jump like a frog and was almost as fast as my friends. It took me a long time to find out that never ever giving up was more important than winning.

When I was about to leave the hospital, I got my first cat and many more after that. All my childhood cats helped me tremendously, cheered me up and made me a happy-happy girl. I could talk to them and they never betrayed me. They knew all my secrets and sorrows which I confided to them alone. I also told them all the fairy tales I made up.

Whenever one of my intimate friends died, it made me cry terribly. And they died very often of cat's disease, because at that time—in the 1930s—nobody knew anything about vaccination. Besides, we wouldn't have had the money to treat our cats. Father worked for a chocolate factory where they kept cats because of all the mice. Every year, he brought a new kitten home—not at all to the delight of my mother. Each time a new 'kitty' arrived, she became quite hysterical because she had just about recovered from the last 'troublesome' cat who had died. But I remember well how happy I was about each new arrival, especially after all those tears I had just shed for the former cat.

At that time, I ignored my handicap completely. I was a happy-happy girl—a little clown—especially at school. I was full of mischief and made people laugh. Father sometimes called me 'Sunny Boy'. Well, I looked like a boy because of my short haircut… and I behaved like a boy. My parents told me that before my illness I had been a shy little birdie, always hanging around my mother's skirts with a piping, little voice.

Another child—a tomboy with a loud, rough voice—left the hospital.

How proud I was that, on my bicycle, I was faster than everybody else although I had only one leg to pedal with. And poor Puss—whether she liked it or not—had to come for a ride with me once in a while.

But trying out my sister's skis wasn't such a success story. When I came back from the hospital, my biggest worry was, would I ever be able to ski? 'Of course, Darling – later!' Mom said and I couldn't understand why she was crying. Well, 'Darling's' first trial ended in an apple tree. Everybody was laughing. Bitterly disappointed and in tears, I went home, dragging my wooden failure behind me. Why had my mother lied to me? At that moment, I realised that there must be many other things I dreamed of that I would never be able to achieve. Holding Puss in my arms, I sat in a corner for a long time. I never tried skiing again.

Dad understood my misery and to cheer me up he gave me a violin. How

I hated the daily practice on this martyr of an instrument, to fiddle boring études while my sister played football and announced proudly to all the world that I was about to give a Cats Concert. I could have strangled her, because I would have so much preferred to play outside too. But as Dad had scratched together his last pennies to buy me this violin, I kept on fiddling and Puss listened patiently to my miserable tunes.

•••••

I was about sixteen, when I shed tears for days—and most nights—because Punky, my dearest cat friend,

apparently had disappeared. Some time later I realised that Mother had given him away behind my back. The reason for this, in my view, absolutely disgusting act was—and I remember it as if it had happened yesterday—that 'Punky-dear' had forgotten his good manners. We had just sat down to lunch when he disappeared in the corner behind the radio and did what he obviously needed to do, right there and then. (He did have a box filled with shredded pages from the telephone directory but he didn't seem to like it much.) After certain unmistakable noises from Punky—and

by taking away my only 'heart friend', she would not have removed Punky. After that incident, I turned nasty and stubborn—displaying much worse behaviour than the usual teenage blues. I am sure a nice smoochy cat would have improved my mood a lot. But no more cats were allowed. So the shy 'birdie' wanted to come back once in a while. But I said: 'No dear, that's no good place for you to stay! Please, fly away, fly outside into the garden, where there are many trees and flowers for you!'

•••••

What followed were years of struggle, saving money for operations to get rid of the odious iron chains on my leg and finally travel and work all over the world. After being an au pair in England, I chopped nuts in a chocolate factory in Sweden, typed letters in Paris, went to school in Spain, hitch-hiked to Denmark and finished up in the United States typing itineraries in a travel agency in San Francisco, working very hard. Finally I had enough pennies in my stocking to go off travelling around the world 'on a shoestring'—towards adventure, and unforgettable impressions. Amidst all this beauty, however, there were many moments when I longed to caress a cat's fur.

a foul smell spreading quickly—my whole family left the table, screaming their heads off in horror and shouting at me. (The poor cat suffered from diarrhoea, but in those days a cat was not supposed to be sick and there were no vets around!) The spaghetti got cold and I was ordered to clean up because it was my cat. I tried to do so, but alas, got sick from the smell in the radio corner. Mother then tried to clean up the mess. But she got sick too and finally had to clean up for the three of us.

That was the end of my last, beloved childhood cat. I still think that if Mother had known what she was doing to me

Finally, after all these years of gypsy-life, I settled back in Switzerland in a dear little home with lots of green around it. 'You need a companion in your pretty place' my friends insisted. I looked at my brand new designer sofa, for which I had scraped together every penny, thought of the dirt, fur and scratches… 'No', I insisted, 'no way'.

But my protests were useless. Soon after, a wet, dripping shoe-box was brought to me. With a teeny-weeny mewling, eight-week-old bit of fluff: a darling of a black-and-white puss, looking with frightened, begging eyes through a peep-hole in the box. 'Here I am, take me out of this horrible place, miaow.' Instantly the cats had my life back.

•••••

Many years have passed since that day. I have become an old cookie of seventy-seven years with lots of little woe-woes. I don't care, dancing is over anyway! I am glad that I had to learn very early to accept life as it comes and to always make the best of every day. Looking back I think I didn't do too badly, although it was not easy—my 'handicapped' life. But I had a many-coloured, thrilling, fascinating and not-boring time! And—of this I'm convinced—without my velvet-paws, my four-padded friends, leaving paw prints on my heart and bringing so much pleasure and fun into my life, I never, never could have managed it so well.

Liselotte Lässig *was born 1925 in Switzerland, and lived in Kilchberg, home of Lindt & Sprüngli chocolate and near the beautiful Lake of Zurich. Although attacked by polio at the age of five which left her with a paralysed leg, Liselotte struggled through life quite successfully, travelling the world and working as a travel consultant for over twenty-five years. After her retirement she lived in an old, little schoolhouse in the south of France, travelling back and forth to Switzerland, always in the company of her cats. Now they live happily in a lovely place back home that overlooks her dear lake and snowy mountains, remembering the many adventures and unforgettable souvenirs in her life including her many cat companions.*

Giving Life Purr-Puss

Marilyn Mitchell

I suffer from schizophrenia which makes relationships with others difficult. The exception is my cat, a special and successful relationship.

We have been together for ten years, since she was just a kitten and the runt of the litter. During that time, women have come into my life, then gone again. But with Jerie, the bond has remained firm. It was love-at-first-sight and is love-continuing on both sides, if her attachment and affection are anything to go by.

Ironically, Jerie came into my life when I was off my face and having a psychotic episode. It was a warm summer day and I was manic and restless with the heat. I was hearing voices. They eventually guided me to dress up and go up-town to a classy pet store. There, they guided me as I looked in the window at a litter of kittens. Naturally they advised me that the docile, wobbly one would be the one best suited to my quiet, reclusive personality rather than the cute and frisky ones which would be too hyperactive for my lifestyle. The schizophrenic voices or auditory hallucinations often make a lot of sense, contrary to popular expectation.

In a manic state, one often does startling things with money. On this occasion (and with three school-aged children at home in my care) I had $400 to pay the electricity and telephone bills. But the voices told me to arrange deferment of these as a pedigree pet was the priority.

I entered the premises. I was very formal and spoke in monosyllables. The two shop girls looked at one another with concern (my manner may have seemed eccentric to them). I simply pointed to the kitten chosen for me and said, 'That one.' They hesitated for a few moments, uncertain as to whether they should give it to me. Was I, perhaps, a crazed cat-killer? (This mostly incorrect equation of violence with mentally-ill people is not unusual among ordinary people.) I would have looked very serious. Eventually, they fetched the little ginger ball of fluff, but the atmosphere was still tense.

That is, until they placed the little sweetheart into my cupped hands. Then I could not help but break my mask-like expression into a very broad smile. They looked again at one another, apparently relieved that I was okay with the kitten. I received the papers (she was half Persian and half Burmese), handed over the best $400 I've ever spent and carried my prize on my lap all the way home.

Cats do not discriminate against disability. They care only that you are kind and good to them. They are sensitive and responsive and easy to please—a strip of beef here or a chin-tickle there. And how they enjoy your company! Whether curled up on a corner of your bed while you are reading or sitting on your lap in front of the television.

Meal times are always for two at our place, now that my children have grown up and left home. Jerie and I have a good life together, as I mostly work from home and don't go out much. We are growing old together. She is now ten and I am half a century.

I know what she likes—and give it to her! Tuna is her favourite food and lean strips of beef, plus a few biscuits to nibble on in-between. Occasionally, she will go outside for a while to sit in the garden, though she never leaves the

yard. Generally, she prefers to be indoors—which suits me just fine. Because she is petite, the birds squawk and dive-bomb her. I tell her that she's supposed to chase them—it's our private joke. And she starts to purr.

Pet therapy is definitely effective. Jerie is forever grateful—as I am for her—and she is never ill-tempered. A teacher by profession, I naturally talk to her and she understands a plethora of words: fish, pooh, mummy, birdies, pussy cat, 'Get 'em!' (cockroaches and flies)—and more. We are devoted companions in a life that otherwise might be problematic for both of us.

Marilyn Mitchell is fifty-one years old, an educator and has three grown-up children. She enjoys reading—especially poetry—art exhibitions and nature. She has had schizophrenia since 1979, and her cat Jerie has contributed massively to her quality of life.

Allergy Claire Pickard

My husband was an optimistic man. He had to be, or he would never have married me.

It was obvious from the first that we were ill suited. He wanted a large house in the suburbs, neighbours to impress, and weekends on the golf course.

I loathed the suburbs, didn't give a damn about the neighbours but was more than happy for him to spend his weekends on the golf course. We married because he had money and I needed it.

The wedding gave a fair indication of the ways things stood. He wanted a lavish affair; I was ashamed and wanted as little fuss as possible. Fortunately, this was construed as bridal embarrassment and I gave a passable performance on the day.

His choice of honeymoon location was a pleasant surprise. I had anticipated a ghastly American trip on which he could play golf amid the palms, but he suggested Scotland. Golf among the heather suited me more. We went on walks. I feigned interest when he attempted to teach me how to play, and I won some time to myself through the expedient of starting a holiday journal.

Writing filled my husband with awe. It was something he failed entirely to comprehend. It also happened to be something that obsessed me. Hence my need for an unearned income.

After the honeymoon, we returned to our house in the suburbs and fell into a routine. When he had left for work, I would settle myself at my desk, light myself a cigarette, and start to write. After he returned, we would eat together, talk for a while, and as soon as I decently could, I would absent myself and write some more.

Things continued in this way for some months. Whilst I could not say that we were happy, neither would I say that we were

miserable. Then, one week in June, everything fell apart.

It must have been about ten o'clock in the morning. I had been writing for an hour or so when I saw him jump up onto the windowsill. He was large, ginger, and distinctly the worse for wear. His ears were torn, his nose was scarred and his fur was matted. We exchanged a long glance. Then, he settled down on his haunches and I went back to work. He stayed there for the rest of the morning, just watching me write. He seemed fascinated by the process.

When it was time for lunch, I made myself a sandwich and walked out into the garden. He jumped down off the sill and sauntered up to me. I offered him a piece of sandwich. He sniffed delicately at it, separated the bread from the cheese and sampled the latter. When he had finished, he marched straight into the house and curled up on the sofa. He spent the afternoon asleep.

My husband returned at 7 o'clock. From the first, he failed to appreciate Ginger's charm. The words 'mangy' and 'fleabag' were spoken. He insisted Ginger must go, I insisted he must stay. Ginger fled in the ensuing row. I stormed off to bed.

The following morning, Ginger returned. This time I let him straight into the house. He spent the morning asleep in the armchair beside my desk. At lunchtime, I provided tuna fish and milk. As soon as he heard my husband's key in the door, he ran out into the garden and vanished over the fence.

This pattern continued for the rest of the week. Ginger would arrive in the morning, stay with me throughout the day, and leave as soon as my husband returned. Relations between my husband and myself remained frosty. I installed a calendar featuring ginger cats in the kitchen. He snorted in contempt when he saw it.

Outwardly, we had reached stalemate. Yet my husband was unaware of the development that had taken place in

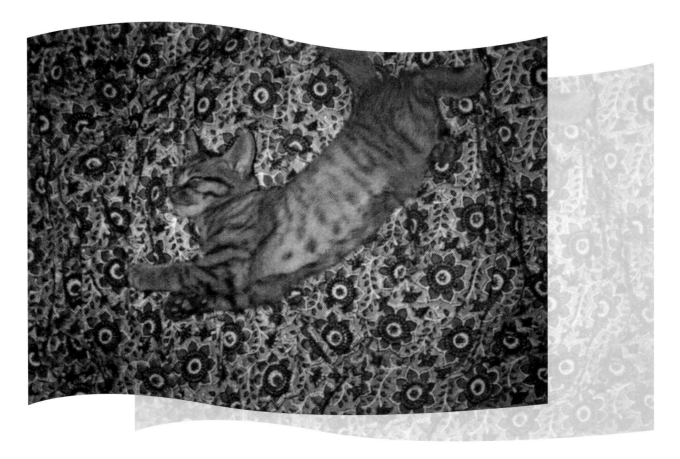

my relationship with Ginger. His torn ears and scarred face were now beautiful in my eyes. His matted fur, now lovingly combed by myself, was silken to my touch. In short, I was besotted.

On Friday morning, I woke to the sound of my husband gasping for breath. By the time the ambulance came, he was unrecognisable. His face was red and swollen, his eyes barely visible in the puffy flesh. Apparently, he had suffered a severe allergic reaction. Ginger was almost certainly the cause. When he heard the news, he patted my hand and tried to smile, 'I'm sorry love, he really will have to go.'

My husband was released three days later. No doubt he was surprised, when I wasn't there to meet him. And no doubt he was alarmed when he returned home to find our house empty. But I can't quite picture his reaction when he found the note I had left on the sofa, in the spot where Ginger liked to sleep. No, I can't quite imagine his reaction when he read the words, 'He's gone—So have I.'

Claire Pickard is studying English literature in Oxford, UK. She has known and loved many cats over the years. However, she has only recently acquired one of her own—an extremely handsome ginger tom named Hilary.

Pia and Zami

Orange Biscuit Conchita Fonseca

I was to discover
the wonderful sound of a kitten's purr,
an amazing fold in her kitten ear –
the velvet softness of kitten fur,
orange gold stripes like a tiger's
and her button nose!

My name is Conchita Bernadette Annalise Usha Fonseca. My family migrated from India in 1967. I am an Indian of French, Portuguese heritage. I grew up in Geelong, Victoria and although many of my friends had pets during their childhood, apart from a few goldfish, our home was pet deprived. During my first years in Australia many of my schoolmates would ask me about leaving my pets behind in India. I would tell stories of a baby elephant and chimpanzee, my fingers crossed tightly behind my back. Above all else, I wanted to belong—and my head was filled with imaginings of animal friends but it was to be a long time before I was introduced to the pleasures of an orange tabby, named Scout.

I came to live in Melbourne in 1992, after ten years in Brisbane. I was recovering from an automobile accident. I had no job and very few friends, and although my parents lived an hour's drive away from Melbourne, I felt alone.

She came into my life at a time when I was uncertain of my future, insecure and shy. Crawling under the fence of a Fitzroy vet and into my heart, a teeny ball of orange fluff, determined green eyes and sizeable silky paws—she would be named 'Scout.' The name was used by Harper Lee in her novel *To Kill a Mockingbird* for the strong-willed, intelligent, steadfast and courageous Scout Finch.

Scout's arrival filled me with wonder and trepidation. I gazed for hours at this little creature as she tripped over her own paws, exploring her new home.

It was 'love at first sight' and everywhere I walked, Scout followed close behind. I moved nervously about—unsteady on my feet, with the aid of my walking cane—afraid that if I stumbled and fell, she would be hurt.

At night I would lay awake as Scout, having crawled onto the precarious position on my shoulder, slept soundly. I feared that I would fall asleep, roll over and squash her, however this little kitten was adventurous, agile, determined and quick. She would be my character reverse, yet complement—she would draw me out, make me challenge my physical abilities and become the protagonist in my discovery of new friendships, aspirations and goals.

Scout, like myself, has not been spared the pain of physical injury. When she was four, while playing with her cat-mate Black Black she fell out of a large silky-oak tree and suffered a broken pelvis. Absurdly, this was one of my injuries in the car accident a few years before and while she was trapped in a cage, immobilised for a month, we bonded even more. Scout would learn to walk again, just as I had.

It would take Scout several months to heal and for a short time we shared a matching limp and both walked with difficulty!

Both our lives have changed greatly in our twelve years together. We have moved houses and I have changed jobs. We have grown older and wiser. We've met many wonderful women and their cats and dogs, and we've grown especially close to some.

We now share much of our time with Zami, Pia and my partner Jane. Zami, a chocolate Burmese, is insightful, protective and strong-willed. Pia, her little 'sister' is the colour of milk coffee, comical and intensely affectionate.

We travel from town house to beach house, three cats in tow, meowing and yawning in the back of Jane's wagon.

My Scout, lovingly called 'Orange Biscuit' by Jane—has two new playmates. The three can often be found curled up together in front of the fire or chasing each other noisily down the long corridor of our Victorian terrace. They roll in the sunshine, cuddle up and join in the usual squabbling, which occurs between siblings. For me there is always that constant meow for food, and a warm friend to snuggle or comfort. There are now stories to share, moments to capture on film—adventures to experience and record. There is hope, challenge and laughter. We are a family of the 21st century. Our lives are filled with joy and passion more so for the love of our cats.

Conchita Fonseca was born into a creative family, and worked for many years as a chef/manager in Geelong, Brisbane and Melbourne. Now with time to take pleasure in the finer things, she is discovering a career as an artist. Her life is made richer with the companionship of three cats.

Scout

Little Cat's Melody
Fide Erken

a little sleeping cat
more than sweet
an old melody
bringing a beautiful memory

little cat was invited
by the fairy of wonderland
there she met
other little cats
they slept then danced
hearing the same melody

it was a little children's song
i sang when i had a little cat
it brings me my cat's memory
but it's hard to believe
that my cat also sings it
in cats' wonderland
and remembers me

don't cry little girl
your sweet is also there
and singing the same melody

Küçük Kedilerin Melodisi

uyuyan küçük kedi
sevimli mi sevimli
güzel bir anıyı canlandıran
eski bir melodi

kediler ülkesinin perisi
küçük kediyi davet etti
orada buluştu diğerleriyle
uyudular ve dans ettiler
dinleyerek aynı ezgiyi

küçük çocukların şarkısıydı o
ben de söylerdim
varken küçük bir kedim
bana onu anımsatır
ama kediler ülkesindeki kedimin
onu söyleyip beni hatırladığına inanmak
 zor değil mi?

ağlama küçük kız
senin sevgili kedin de orada şimdi
ve söylemekte aynı ezgiyi

Fide Erken is a Turkish woman aged thirty-six. She work as an English teacher in Turkey. Writing poems in Turkish and Engish takes a big and a beautiful part in her life. She sends all her love to the world people with her poems.

Monkey Lucy Sussex

These events all happened a long time ago, but in memory they still are raw…

We can be absurdly grateful for small acts of help, or grace, such as the stranger who provides directions on an unfamiliar university campus, or gives you a banana when you are faint from lack of blood sugar and having a tough time with US immigration officials. Conversely, we can be absurdly resentful for small acts of malice or spite, remembered bitterly for many years after the event. And perhaps rightly, because people show their true selves at such moments. I am absurdly grateful to a small seal-point Siamese cat called Monkey, surely beyond all nine lives now. What can you give a cat? Nothing perhaps, but thanks.

A wretched day, the worst in my life. I was unemployed and came home to discover my flatlet had been invaded by a strange, stalking man. He was intent on rape, because I resembled the girl who had jilted him (he said). But he was disconcerted by the fact of menstruation, the mention of which caused him to drop me like a hot stone, and also because I set out to disconcert him. Many years later, I was to find that talking to an assailant, trying to make them see you as a person—just like them, in fact—was recommended procedure in cases of kidnap etc.

So I talked to this creep for three hours, as my mouth dried up and my voice grew hoarse. I got him to leave. Then things really got unpleasant…

His last words had been, 'Don't tell the cops or I'll killya.' Which of course gave me a fixed and terrible determination to do precisely that. The problem was my relatives. They had arranged to take a friend to dinner at a German restaurant and I, with my story, was a terrible inconvenience. I could go to the police afterwards but in the meantime I was to go with them to the restaurant, and not say a thing to their guest. With the result that, in the odd oscillation between trauma and triumph, I drank too much. When I finally got to the police I created an extremely poor impression.

She, not a blood relative, hissed in my ear, 'You sound like a little girl who has made up a story just to get attention.'

One small act of malice, revealing much, never to be forgotten.

One small act of kindness, or whatever it was: at the restaurant was Monkey, who unbidden, despite the catlovers at the table, headed for my lap. He sat there throughout, purring loudly. I have met cats who are anybody's since, but not one who has unerringly selected, from a group of people, the one in need of succour, the small tactile complaisant pleasures of a cat.

Funny, how Monkey was the only one who knew how to treat me.

Lucy Sussex was born in New Zealand in 1957, and works as a researcher, editor, reviewer and writer in various genres. She has edited four anthologies, and her writing has been published internationally. Her novel The Scarlet Rider *won the 1997 Ditmar award. She is currently writing* Cherchez les Femmes, *a study of the first women writers of crime and mystery fiction.*

Gypsy

Anne Quain

Gypsy came to our home when my mother was pregnant. She slipped in through the broken palings at the forbidden part of our backyard in Wallsend and wouldn't leave.

A persistent little grey tabby with an unrelenting meow, she would plant herself firmly on my expectant mother's bulge, and knead. Gypsy could feel me kicking, and I am certain that I was soothed by that deep purr reverberating in my mother's womb.

Ex utero, it was a connection I took for granted. Gypsy was moody and prone to turning on you, delivering spectacular scratch marks in unlikely places (nostrils were a favourite).

It was only several years later, when we moved to a new home in Stockton, that we learned she was epileptic. I was five when she had her first seizure. I was standing in the

bathroom when my mother began to scream. Petrified, I watched as Gypsy rolled into the room, clawing and yowling and spasming in a ball of chaos. I bawled my eyes out as she tore out her fur and bled on the white tiles. After a few minutes she collapsed in exhaustion, and so did we.

In spite of medication, she became even moodier. I couldn't understand why my friends were reluctant to touch her. A bite or a scratch was never personal, after all. They would laugh at me when Gypsy growled. I didn't think I was any different, but I was told I was a 'cat person'. It would be years before I discovered the meaning of this honour.

I was fifteen when Gypsy was put down by the steely-looking Mr Smith, our vet. Arthritis, incontinence, weight loss… I remember mum trying to justify the 'right decision'. It seemed grossly unfair that I was at school

when she died. My cheeks were burning with tears as our family congregated in the back yard where she was buried that afternoon.

The loss was not unexpected— months before she deteriorated, we had an influx of potential replacements. Strays started dropping in and testing the food, our laps. They gave Gypsy a wide berth and got down to negotiating rent with my father, who was In Charge.

A brown tabby kitten proved the most persuasive, and moved in immediately. And so the pattern continued until I moved to Sydney to complete an arts degree.

Life in the city proved expensive and complicated. The woman I boarded with suffered from rheumatoid arthritis. In the evenings when we talked she would point her gnarled fingers at me and tell me that you could catch it from kissing cats. In the mornings I would share my Milo with the neighbour's cat. It seemed we were both starved for a nameless bond.

I chose philosophy as a major and immersed myself in academia, constantly reading and writing essays about the good life. I adored Spinoza, whose metaphysics gave a place to every life-form: 'We are all modes of the one existence…' and made sense of the world. I was buoyed by the encouragement of my lecturers and pegged my self-esteem on a diet of high distinctions.

I moved into a share-house and met Lambie. Actually, I hadn't noticed him until I felt those claws in my leg. 'Oh, he's an aggressive little shit,' hissed my future flatmate. I noticed that his bottom lip was permanently curled out, and wondered if someone had punched him in the face.

We spent every night in bed together… until I met Chris. We were

mismatched from the start but I clung to him for reasons I still cannot fathom. Perhaps it was his wandering eye that fuelled my need to be with him—and not to be without him. I moved out and left Lambie to the mercy of the housemates.

In hindsight, this lack of judgement signalled the beginning of the depression that I spiralled into. It was my honours year, my academic record gave every indication that I was on the road to the University Medal. I had published in international journals at age twenty-one. I thought I was a star.

Then one morning I woke up and didn't want to get out of bed or leave the house. I cried all day. I starved myself. The next day was the same. I was inflamed with inexplicable self-hatred.

At first my family and friends called to jostle me out of it, but after months they, like me, were fed up. I could no longer justify myself to myself. I had given up on completing honours, or anything, ever. Realising how grim things were, Chris moved Lambie into the house with us. With the responsibility of Lamb's little life in my hands, I could not take my own.

Even so I came close. One night yet another crisis counsellor on yet another crisis number paused and asked me: 'What is the smallest unit of happiness you can think of?' I answered touching a cat. He asked me: 'How can you amplify that?' I didn't know. My imagination had evaporated when depression fried my brain. But answers came from somewhere. Animals. Touching animals. Helping animals. Nurse. Vet. Cats. The one given in my life.

Given my history it was surprising that I had made nothing of this connection, but this midnight conversation made sense.

The next day I had the energy to apply for veterinary science. To my astonishment my application was accepted. I wrote my honours thesis in the same week that I read every James Herriot book ever published. Lamb and I moved out. I've not had another high distinction but somehow my life makes sense.

This year I am doing honours again—this time on feline infectious peritonitis. When I think of Gypsy, and I do, often, I wonder if I was chosen—if this chain of events were somehow destined. What I do know is that cats are the point at which I connect with the universe.

Anne Quain *has a bachelor of arts in philosophy, and is currently studying veterinary science at the University of Sydney. She spent eighteen months living above an inner-city vet hospital taking care of patients after hours, and delights in the company of all animals, particularly cats. She writes and takes photographs for veterinary magazines. She currently lives with two moggies (Mike and Lil), and regularly sleeps with her patients.*

Milk

Alison Ritter

I hate being needy—if I let myself need, then it will overtake me, consume me, drown me. So I do away with neediness. With breathtaking omnipotence, I can solve all problems. All that is required is a good action plan. I learn how to tune a car; I get well-educated and work hard at my career; I fix dripping taps; I save money and buy myself a house. I will do anything not to be needy. It is so functional—to be competent, to be clever and effective in this world. And I get promoted and admired for this.

There is perhaps only one downside—it is very hard to have a relationship with someone who has no needs. It is impossible to be around someone, intimately around them, when they need nothing from you. So there is just me and my cat, Tess, the one constant relationship.

There is something wrong with this absence of need, and hence psychoanalysis begins. And I struggle—hah, I don't need analysis! But I go to the couch every day. I struggle to grasp that analysis is not like an action plan, where you identify the problem, prioritise the key strategic areas, work through each one systematically and tick them off the list. Analysis is a relationship where yesterday a story had one meaning, next week it will have another one altogether, next month it will be forgotten and next year it will return as a new story.

My cat Tess absolutely loves milk, and she would cry for it every day. As a kitten she used to get the leftover milk from the breakfast cereal bowls, but that stopped many years ago. I look back and think that my beautiful and well-loved constant companion cried for milk every morning.

And every morning I said 'no'. Because she was too needy. If I gave in, she would have milk in the morning and then want milk every night and then during the day and it would never stop. It would consume her, devour her. And she would drown in milk because of her neediness. Ah—this is what happens when you are needy and let it be met—you will want more and more and it will overwhelm you.

I can't remember when the story of Tess and her daily crying for milk came to my analysis—but there it was. A story about neediness—my cat's neediness for milk and my insistence that this need not be met.

So one day I gave Tess milk. She was just delighted. She loves milk. And she hasn't been devoured. She has not drowned. For the last few years every morning Tess has her milk. She is sixteen years old now—with no sign of ageing, a playful, loving companion who licks the milk from her whiskers every day. And I am still in analysis, with everchanging stories. It is never, or perhaps not even as simple as just learning to give your cat milk.

Alison Ritter is thirty-nine years old and lives alone with her two cats—Tess (sixteen years old), and Jerry (seven years old). She has always had cats in her life—from her childhood pet (Twinkle Toes) to now and she loves them to pieces. She works as a researcher in addictions, with a clinical psychology background.

Anna
Jacqueline Crompton Ottaway

Through the chemotherapy

Anna lies beside her

places a tortoiseshell paw across her body

purrs   snuggles closer

her eyes fill with compassion

uncertainty.

When the chemotherapy ends

Anna stretches

throws her a look that says

'You're going to be okay now'

then wanders off

to seek her favourite spot

in the sun.

Jacqueline Crompton Ottaway has had poems, prose and children's stories published in New Zealand and overseas. She was also the winner of the Commonwealth Short Story Competition for the Pacific region in 2000 and lives in Auckland in a state of chaos with her husband, three children and two cats.

Myfanwy

Karen Atkinson

It is the brown eye you notice first, then the tail held hard and erect in the air like a call to battle. There's nothing gracious in her movement; with Fanny it's just firm strides, her back rigid and her nose in the air. She arches and stretches against the calf of my leg and instinctively my hand moves out to stroke her. The caress is received with forbearance, something that must be done if the meal is to be dished up on time. She knows the protocol, I know mine. I remind myself that I am of the privileged few, the small elite that can touch her. Unsolicited intimacy brings a spitting, biting response guaranteed to put off the most avid of cat lovers. She's consistent in that; I warn all newcomers to watch their p's and q's, no gestures of fond familiarity for this putty tat.

It wasn't always like that. Myfanwy, Fanny for short, comes into my life soft and cuddly. Kittenish exuberance melts my heart. My love is unconditional. And unrequited.

Who can say when a malleable ball of tortiseshell fur, a beloved pet, individuates. Begins calling the shots. Pushing the buttons. Perhaps it is in the adolescent years that her identity as a female of independent spirit is vigorously asserted. Before I can say Cat Ballou she is proud, arrogant even, and determined to shun all the outward displays of submission inherent in the usual role of domestic pet.

I guess I have only myself to blame. It is the seventies and I yearn for liberation. While my sisters and I are reading Greer and Steinem, consciousness raising and burning our bras, Fanny is living it. While we vow to uncross our legs and practice looking at our vaginas in make-up mirrors, lack of modesty becomes her calling card. While we analyse and bitch, Fanny struts around, wholly actualised, totally liberated. While we talk the talk, she walks the walk.

Her name is no accident. I bestow the name Myfanwy in the symbolic fervour of a feminist intent on reclaiming the female body. We roll rude words around on our tongues, explore possibilities and claim for our own, our bodies and the words used to describe them. And to denigrate them. 'Cunt, course slang, female genitals, unpleasant person.' Not for us. We celebrate the old term, the cunny of ancient godessess, of the sisters who had lived and loved before us. Like a banner, a torch, cunny represents each woman story lost. Each woman symbol torn down. Each woman disenfranchised, masculinised.

Resentment sets in; I want revenge. It does not take long for Fanny to be

called by the other derivatives. Rather than celebrating the female form, I find myself abusing her with the more common usage. The window is left ajar to accommodate her nocturnal activity, of which there is lots. On cold wet nights, she scratches and pushes at the covers until I make room for her in the best bit of the dry warm bedding. Other nights she is out on the prowl, picking up who knows who with impunity, while I toss and turn in monogamy and wonder if I will ever meet the man to fire up my G-spot.

Guilt, co-dependence, the burnt chop, these are concepts far from Fanny's concerns. Never one to put herself in the shoes of others, she is indifferent, indeed unaware that there are any needs beyond those of her own. She looks carefully at me, with unblinking yellow glass eyes. Debriefing in the circle helps, but does not take away the feelings of jealousy I have towards my feline sister.

In the eighties when my marriage has disintegrated and life in more urban landscapes beckons, I leave Fanny. I cannot bear to think of her locked in by the city. Like all sisters, we grow into our separate journeys. She retires to life on the farm, while I take my first footsteps into self. I never knew her fate. In my mind she still strides out there, though that would make her one hundred and forty-five cat years old. She seems inviolable, wild femme chosen by the goddess.

*Born and raised in rural WA, **Karen Atkinson** now spend her time between Broome in the north west and Denmark in the lower south. She loves the contrast in the colours of the landscape and the people. Taking time off from a career in education, she is currently working on her first novel.* 🐾

The Departure

Patricia Best

The woman rose early, she could not sleep. The day was already blood hot. It would be a scorcher. She went to the kitchen to make coffee, running the water quietly so it would not make a noise, for it was only four o'clock, and the rest of the family were asleep. She sat in the chair in the shadowy velvet dark, the blood warmth enveloping her, making her aware of her own blood which pounded and beat from her heart slowly. The house felt strange, a part of its life was no longer there, but had left a faint imprint of what was before. The image left on the washed out negative of film.

A large cat pads down the passageway, and bumps his head against her knee. He too had spent a sleepless vigil beside the window ledge. Looking out, waiting for that familiar step. For two nights it had not come. He was puzzled. Not too puzzled though for food. Fed by tasty tit-bits by the bright young girl from kittenhood, he appreciated the pleasure that food brought. Affection, food. The consequence of which he was rather fat, a blue-eyed cream-and-brown cat, a smoky pear of pleasure.

The mother fed him now, and he ate in the way of his ancestors, as the wild lion eats, tearing at his prey, looking up, dragging it to another spot. The cat, though domesticated, had not lost his original nature. But that other side of him—the domesticated—still hungered, and from that hunger, he could find no ease.

He stretched his brown, broad legs, and bumped his head against the woman, looking at her with a miaow. She scratched his short ears, as he rubbed himself against her, and against the chair.

'What's up, Puss?' the woman said, knowing very well.

She scratched his neck, and he stretched it out, so she could reach it better. He miaowed and talked again.

'Missing her eh?' Puss assented. She caressed his silky coat.

The woman remembered. Two days ago, saying goodbye at the plane. The girl has spent the previous week, tidying up her room, sweeping away her childhood into bags; some, very few, for keeping, the rest to be given away. The cat had watched and, as his familiar, untidy habitat had changed, he had retreated to beneath the mother's bed. On the day of the flight, he would not come out to say goodbye. The girl had to call to him under the bed. But he knew and would not come. So she had left without his farewell. The mother, when she said hers, kept a brave face, and hugged her daughter, as family and friends said goodbye. A nineteen-year-old young woman, off to the big smoke to start a new job and career. It was right and natural, but oh, there was an ache, molten and glowing in the mother's chest, which simmered up and flared, so that now she could not sleep.

Fierce love, how strong this could be, startling. All those protective instincts had to be re-arranged. Life is in flux, constantly changing. The lovely girl was now a woman, eager for new sights and experiences. Independence was a glory. The mother knew this, and remembered it. The excitement of reaching out on your own, aware of one's own power. She had left home even younger than her daughter; it

had been such an adventure, challenging, especially the hard times. She knew her daughter would manage and do well. So all was as it should be?

The cat reached up his paws, placing them on her knee. Delicate. Sharp sheathed softness. She rubbed his head, feeling a knot. She smiled at the remembrance of the long suffering cat, patiently stretched out, wide blue eyes looking at the girl as she combed and groomed—the tugging worth the attention. The mother would have to take over the task of grooming that long coat. She caressed the cat's shoulders. His purr, which had thundered so for the girl, now softly began to rumble and grow, his large pawed feet kneading, his purr large, reverberating.

Echos...

In the darkness before dawn, she could feel the room, devoid of its bright presence, the image lingering. As the sun came up, a molten ball on a hot day, the woman and the cat in the kitchen sat for a time and comforted each other.

Patricia Best is a writer and filmmaker. She lives in Adelaide, South Australia, along with partner Jim and son Toby (daughter Katinka now in the UK) together with her two cats Paddington and Wingley, her dog Pendragon and eight pekin bantams. (She once had a rooster called Cecil but that's another story!). Her love for animals, and the joy, wisdom and companionship they bring, features strongly in her life and work.

Home is Where My Cat Lives— or Tabby Consistency

Lavender

In Western Queensland, after the 1950 floods, everything grew at great pace and to great height in our garden and the surrounding paddocks. In the late afternoons, my father would come in from working with the stock and he and my mother would 'get stuck into the garden' for an hour or so before dinner. I had just started correspondence lessons and, after being tied to the school table, and in the care of the governess most of the day, was keen to talk with my parents. They were keen for me to put the pulled weeds into the wheelbarrow.

Some evenings, a tabby cat appeared outside the fence watching this activity, just sitting, then would silently slip away into the long, curly Mitchell grass. We already had an old black-and-white cat, but his evening chore was to keep watch on the kitchen door around the other side of the house. Soon the tabby came into the yard and claimed a spot under the pepper tree. I would leave him meat scraps and gradually he allowed me to hand-feed and stroke him. Thus Mignonette, the gardeners' cat, became part of the household. He slept on my bed and he was my special friend. If I went out in the paddocks, he would wait at the back gate, on top of the fence post for my return. His greatest act of devotion was to bring mice to my room and play with them by my bed.

After a few years, I was sent off to boarding school, and when the class teacher asked for stories of home, I said that my home was where Mignonette lived. My mother's letters gave news of Mignonette and how he kept the new white cat, Angelo, in line. Coming home for holidays was such excitement. As soon as the car stopped at the back gate, I would rush about looking for Mignonette, soon to be found by the pepper tree or in front of the stove in winter. When our home was burnt down, we lived away for over a year as we rebuilt, and my big worry was for Mignonette. All I could think of was going home to see him. Then the time came to move back, and my ten year-old heart burst with joy to be with Mignonette again. Now I was at home with my cat. A few years later, while I was away at school, Mignonette succumbed to a brown snake, and he was buried under the orange tree. Great sadness followed, and my feeling of home changed.

My mother's letters still contained cat tales, however; a couple of strays had been caterwauling about the sheds, and she named them after the governor and his wife who had visited the district recently. When I got home for holidays there was Lady May's litter of kittens to play with. I choose a tabby—Thomas Tiddles—who was almost a replica of Mignonette. I returned to school dreaming of a tabby cat waiting for me at home. In lower

secondary school the girl talk was of clothes, pop songs, and films, but I persisted with stories of my cat who could hunt huge rabbits and frighten off visiting dogs. At night in the dormitory, while other girls talked about boys or parties, I spent many hours thinking of that tabby cat and wishing for a warm lump on my feet called Tommie Tiddles. I was becoming too old to be homesick, but home was where my cat lived.

Tabby consistency continued through the years. I finished school, went on to university, then my first job as a physiotherapist and, whenever I came home, Thomas was always there. He would just appear out of the saltbush hedge by the back gate. When I left to travel and work 'overseas' (as we called it then), I took a photo of Tommie in my wallet to remind me of home. In London, as I was settling into life in a Hammersmith flat, a little tabby cat would hang about the back door. I called her Jennie and my flat-mates thought me soft, as I heated her milk and gave her fish fingers! After work I would walk home through the cold grey winter nights to be met by Jennie. Even if I'd had a night at the opera or the pub, the little tabby would be waiting. Now it was my turn to write cats tales in letters to my mother. I could not adopt Jennie, as I would be moving on, but until then I knew my home was where the tabby cat lived.

Lavender was born in the bush although has lived most of her life in large cities and regional centres—where ever she goes there's always a cat or two. She has worked in hospitals, the public service, the private sector, community services and universites. Since the 1970s she has been active in women's liberation and lesbian politics and community. She was founding mother of Lesbian Network *magazine,* Older Wiser Lesbian Support (OWLS) *and the* Journal of Australian Lesbian Feminist Studies. *Currently she works on the International Women's Day collective each year and is an executive member of the Coalition of Activist Lesbians Australia, a United Nations accredited human rights organisation.*

me

minnie

Minnie and Me

Deb Doyle

Minnie was a small, wizened Gypsy woman I lovingly wrapped and held in a black-fringed shawl patterned with red roses. He growled and cussed, but for me, there was no greater childhood pleasure than to tighten and tuck the shawl's top triangular corner around his head and cradle his minute skull in the crook of my left arm while my other arm pressed his wiry body ever closer to my bosom.

We lived at 14 Dora Street, Eastwood, a northern suburb of Sydney, in a fibro Housing Commission house that's long since gone. From age two and a half to twelve, I lived there with my grandmother and grandfather, and, for a while, with my teenage uncle and aunty. Before I went to live with them, my parents regularly took me there for a visit. As soon as I arrived, I jumped out of the Holden and headed for the barren backyard, in search of Min. Wearing my fashionable nylon dress, I scooped him up in my arms and carried him around until he could make his escape. During one visit, he decided he'd had enough: he clawed me from between my eyebrows to the tip of my nose.

Minnie was the brother and sister I never had. On hot, humid summer days, I tickled his tummy with a piece of paspalum while he purred in ecstasy, the silence broken only occasionally by a blowfly. On the lounge together, he slept in my lap while I watched every TV show from Gidget to The Twilight Zone, in glorious black, white and grey—the same colours as Min's fur. He was usually a good boy, but I once had to pull a pee-wee out of his mouth and tell him he was very naughty. At dinner time, I had to call him only once: '*Minnie-Min-Min-Min-Min-Min-Min-Min-Min! Puddy-Puss-Puss-Puss-Puss-Puss-Puss-Puss-Puss!*'

My little friend contracted cancer of the tail when I was eleven, just before I got my first period. I was at school when he was carted off in a van. I have an indelible image of him: staring out the back window as the van heads towards Booth Street, turns left up to Herring Road, exits right on to the Pacific Highway, and finally stops at a faceless brick clinic, where he's greeted by a man in a white coat. We never got to say goodbye.

Minnie was the first animal I connected with. In childhood, most of the animals I encountered were recently deceased. During trips to the Top Ryde butcher shop with my Nan, I stared at the pig carcasses hanging by hooks along the wall and decided they had to be plastic piggies: people wouldn't kill real ones—would they? One afternoon, I glimpsed the thin, red body of a skinned rabbit wrapped in newspaper on the kitchen sink. I recall my grandmother lamenting, 'Poor little thing.' One night, I cried when she served me up a bowl of rice topped with a fish's head, complete with a blank, lifeless eye staring back at me. What was so different about Min? Why weren't cats strung up by hooks, skinned and wrapped or decapitated and put on rice?

I was twelve when I found out that cats aren't a favoured pet in all cultures. My divorced mother and father reunited briefly for a dinner to celebrate my twelfth birthday at a Chinese cafe. I had trouble cutting through my chicken omelette. The gristle turned out to be a cat's paw. I knew it: it was the same shape as Min's, without the fur. I had the startling realisation that Sylvester the Cat, Bugs Bunny and Porky Pig are one and the same: just like us, but unable to speak.

Deb Doyle is a freelance editor, copywriter, proofreader and editorial-training consultant. She lives in the Melbourne suburb of Brunswick East with her husband Chris, and children Alex, Carlin and Genevieve.

A Cat by Any Other Name...

Susan Wills

I was nine weeks pregnant and in my second year of teacher training. My relationship with the baby's father was emotionally volatile and there was no money.

I think it was around 1983. The movie 'The Right Stuff' had just played in cinemas. There is a scene where Chuck Yeager (the guy who broke the sound barrier in the lead-up to the space race) is striding away from his damaged plane across a heat-hazed tarmac. He removes a helmet alive with burning fuel and doesn't blink. In 1983, this kind of raw courage made me melt.

A plaintive mewing began one night. In the morning, I tracked it down to a tortoiseshell kitten hiding in the jungle of our unkempt backyard. This was a student house. We barely washed dishes. Nectarines rotted where they fell and redback spiders nested in the outdoor loo. The garden had little pathways, much overgrown with weeds and long grass, as well as the sturdier varieties of whichever plants a more-domesticated owner had once sown.

Saucers of milk were fetched and lapped and tiny 'Yeags', named for bravery in the wild, became mine. Sleeping on my bed, the constant humbuzz of her purr was soulfood when the man stayed away for days.

I told no one about the pregnancy. It wasn't going to happen. The termination was arranged and carried out by the requisite twelfth week.

•••••

I was flicking through old photos and found one of myself holding Yeags under the clothesline in that student house. I am wearing the loose indigo dress which I had bought to accommodate my three-month belly.

The photograph recalled the day we learned of Yeags' happenstance. She was the product of a neighbour's cat and earmarked for collection by a father and son. As the pair chatted to our neighbour, Yeags escaped from the box in their car and sought shelter in my garden. She didn't begin her crying until after they had left. They never returned for her.

It was many years before I saw the bittersweet symmetry in that act of fate. Yeags chose to leave the child who wanted her just as I had chosen to lose the child who'd wanted me.

It is too much to say that some quasi-spirit of my unborn child was alive in Yeags. It is not too much to say that in nurturing her, I dealt with that important loss.

Yeags lived with me until I left for overseas. She then went to live with my oldest friend in a rickety house on some rambling acreage in the Adelaide Hills. There she scrambled up and down tall pines and performed dizzying acrobatics. She played the part of 'familiar' to the gypsy-like Benita, the youngest daughter of an eccentric Maltese woman—a wise woman who, with one glance into my eyes, had known about the life I carried in the indigo dress. Benita had just broken up with a musician, and found much solace in Yeags (who she called Yargy). Benita grew more resilient with her tarot and solitude, and was soon ready to move on and leave the rickety house on the hill.

Yeags moved home to live with my mother, who was in the throes of a domestic nightmare with her second and soon-to-be ex-husband. My mother was converted from an ardent cat disliker to a passionate proclaimer of at least one cat's virtues. She still tells of how Yeags once took a swipe at her nemesis, a tormenting tom, as he sat alone in the sun: just to keep him in line. It was out of character for her to attack. It was as if she'd said, 'I know you haven't done anything this time, but just in case, here's one to go on with.' When my mother was ready to reclaim her life, she took a mental swipe at Len and left the house.

My choice of a male name back in 1983 shows how far I've come. Back then, men were strength and courage. Yeags taught me otherwise. She signposted three journeys of courage which all begin with a woman and a walk from a broken dream.

And if I had to name her now? A goddess of strength, like Oya, or Isis, perhaps? Freya sits well. For the three women in this cat tale were blessedly empowered by the magic of a tiny tortoiseshell with a cicada buzzhum purr, the rhythm of which was unfaltering.

Susan Wills *lives, works, mothers, and loves in a Darwin beachside apartment with her partner Andrew and their sons, Nicholas and Henry. She currently has no room for a magical cat though she shares meaningful green-eyed moments with the downstairs-neighbour's black cat when needs arise.*

Go On Mom— You Can Do It! Finola Geraghty

The two cats, who were always more my cats than His, gave me the love and affection that He never could. It's a perfect example of symbiosis—I do my best for them and they purr their thanks back. Each day with them is a gift. Collectively known as The Furry People and known individually as Danni and Max, I don't think I could have managed here without them. He left us two weeks after we moved to a strange country. I knew no one and the pain and panic inside me pulled me down into a deep cavernous low, never before experienced. After each restless night Danni would greet me in the morning in her unique kitty way by rubbing her cold and slightly damp nose in my face. A cat's head has a particular, slightly musky smell, not at all unpleasant. I can still feel her whiskery eyebrows tickling my face. I hope I can still remember it when the cats have become just a memory. Max hasn't quite mastered the social nicety of nose-rubbing, preferring a good strong headbang instead.

When he first saw me cry, he opened his big green eyes in concern. Then he licked his lips, twice. Cats always seem to lick their lips when they are not sure what to do. He looked at his sister as if to say, 'go on, it's a girl thing.' Danni just rubbed her soft, furry body against me while Max silently left the room. I cried a lot after He left us. The Furry People played long and hard to bring a smile to my face. There always seemed to be someone doing something they shouldn't. Entertainment was provided in house and the television became redundant. I used to count the hours until it was time to go home and see them. I have always imagined that, although they don't understand a word I say, they know when I am down. Somehow, they always seem to know when I need comforting. They gave me the spirit and encouragement to carry on when I thought I couldn't, or didn't want to. They relied on me and forced me to function. Slowly, I realised

that I had to start living again. It was all right to turn towards daylight and to smile.

The Furry People couldn't be more different from each other. He has black fur with tabby stripes and an incredible sheen. His perfectly symmetrical long white whiskers and rather earnest green eyes add to his aristocratic demeanour. She, on the other hand, is much smaller, has very thick fur not dissimilar to a teddy bear and has a robust playful personality. 'Look at me, I'm here. How can you not take notice of me?' She follows me around faithfully and it is not so much that she is my cat, but more that I am her human. Maybe it's just a girl thing.

They are like the person I am and the person I would like to be. Max is nervous, quiet and waits patiently. He doesn't like getting into trouble so if his sister steals food, he will only eat it if it drops onto the floor. He always loiters at the back, never wanting to stand out too much. Danni, on the other hand, would be of true benefit to the Socialist movement—what's yours is mine. I wish I could throw away my inhibitions and enjoy life the way she does. If something doesn't come to you, then it's easy, just help yourself. Reach out and grab with both hands whatever it is that you desire. If you believe in yourself you can do it.

Finola Geraghty *is a biologist and spent seven years working as a research fellow in London, UK. In May 2002 she moved to Düsseldorf, Germany with her two cats and is now enjoying a slightly less hectic lifestyle. Currently, Finola works for a German biotechnology company.*

Serendipity

Diane Helliker

I believe cats to be spirits
come to earth
A cat, I am sure could
walk on a cloud without
coming through.
Jules Verne.

August 1960

The resident barn cat had a litter of five. 'Please Grandpa, can I have one? Please—Pretty p-l-e-a-s-e.' 'We'll see,' my grandfather groaned. 'I'll talk to your mother.' I ran into the kitchen to tell Grandma about the adorable kittens. 'Free to a Good Home, that's what the sign read. Please Grandma, can I take one home?' I pleaded. 'Your mother doesn't much care for cats, but I'll see what I can do.'

I returned to the barn a few days later. Two kittens were left, one was chocolate brown, the other was orange. I chose the latter, because she looked like Marmalade in the stories. I didn't choose the name Marmalade, I suppose because it was already taken. I called my kitten Snowball. The only white on her was on her front paws. The name suited her just the same. We prepared for the long drive home, north of Toronto.

Four hours later, the car pulled into the driveway. My mother was not pleased to see Snowball. 'It must never go in the house, it will remain outdoors and fend for itself,' my mother warned me. 'What about food, how will she survive?' I asked. 'We barely have enough for ourselves, I can't buy cat food. There are enough mice around, it'll survive. That's how the cats lived on the farm. They weren't pets. They were workers, they kept the mice at bay.' I jumped in, 'I'll use my allowance to buy cat food.' My mother continued, 'Then it will lose the incentive to hunt for food.'

I placed a bowl of milk in the garage, and put a blanket in a box for Snowball. I spent all of my spare time in the garage with her before school, after school; I wanted to be with her. I worried that she wasn't getting enough to eat, so I snuck food out to her.

October 1960

I came home from school one day, to find the milk bowl full and no sign of my new feline companion. 'Mommy!' I shouted, 'Have you seen Snowball? She is gone.' 'She probably ran away, cats are like that, they're drifters,' my mother replied, rather nonchalantly. I kept night vigils by her box in the garage until I was forced to come in. I ran out every morning hoping she had come home. I missed her so.

Several weeks later, I heard a boy at my school talk about the cats his father captured to serve at his Chinese restaurant. 'The customers don't know the difference from chicken,' he said. I thought of Snowball, and wondered if she was one of

the unfortunate ones to end up in the boiling pot. I felt sick to my stomach. 'What's wrong with you?' he asked, 'You eat pig, cow, chicken, don't you?' 'Not anymore,' I said.

May 2002

Ottawa, Canada. I am visiting my friend I affectionately call Peony. She has two feline companions, she calls Benvolio and Leo. We are sitting on the couch knitting, sipping Italian wine, and chatting. Leo is sitting behind my head, flirting with me. Ben is asleep across the room. 'You know, you should really get a cat; my boys love you,' Peony said. 'I suppose I could, now that my mother is gone,' I responded.

I suddenly realised how sad it can be when you allow someone to exert so much control, to have so much influence over your life. This is the way it was with my mother and me. She had an intense dislike for animals and still believed until her death in April 2002 that it was absurd to allow a cat into your home and, even more so, to say it was part of your family. I'm ashamed to admit that I was afraid to bring a cat into my life, for fear of losing her love, of displeasing her. All I could do now was move on. Her death had set me free.

I observed Peony with Ben, Leo with Ben, Leo with Peony. I was intrigued, entranced by the special bond between them. The morning I was leaving, I bent down to talk to Ben. Peony wanted to capture our tete-a-tete on film—yet she dared not move—she decided instead to etch this moment in her mind—me wearing the pink hat with flower, Ben looking at me intensely. 'Ben,' I said, 'I am going home to look for a cat. You've helped me make this decision. You, Leo and Peony. I shall always be grateful for this. Thank you.'

July 2002

I read everything about cats I could find. I decided I would like a female, long-hair calico, and I would call her Molly. The website for the Toronto Humane Society showed pictures of the cats available for adoption. I saw her picture on the computer screen. 'Long-hair female calico, nine years. Her name is Molly'. Peony drove to the Humane Society. 'What if someone adopted her? There will

be other cats but I'm drawn to her,' I said. 'Somehow, I doubt it, this a clear case of serendipity, you and Molly are meant to be together,' replied Peony. I moved quickly from cage to cage looking for Molly.

The medical waiver mentioned fur loss, tooth decay, aggression with other cats, refusal to use litter box. I looked at her: she was beautiful, a little the worse for wear. The base of her tail was bald, possibly she chewed the fur off because of the stress of being in a cage. I understood the medical waiver but that didn't change my mind. I wanted her. Molly put her paw through the cage as if to say I want you too.

She has been with me for six months. Her fur grew back on her tail. She needed only teeth cleaning. I asked her vet, 'What does it mean when Molly jumps on my chest and moves her front paws as though she were on a treadmill?' 'It means she is very happy,' he told me. Molly had been with me for eleven days when my father died. The last time I saw him, at the senior's home, I had bought a carrier for Molly and showed it to him. He wondered how we could sleep, with a cat in the house; he seemed afraid of cats.

I was inconsolable after my father's death. Molly and I had already formed a strong bond and she sensed my melancholy. She stayed close by me and would jump on my chest and do the kneading; the more distressed I was, the harder her little paws would work. She occasionally would lick a tear off my cheek, and make a smacking sound, as if the salt was a little hard on her tastebuds. She would sleep in the bed with me, staring, observing, intent. I have learned so much from her. She is a beautiful, gentle creature, so knowing. I don't pine over the years I missed having a feline companion. I am grateful that Molly came into my life at a time when we needed each other.

Diane Helliker lives in Toronto, Canada, with her husband, Douglas, and her cat, Molly. She has a BA in drama and history from the University of Toronto. She writes plays and short stories and reviews books. What she likes about being a writer is that it allows her to spend more time with her precious, feline companion. 🐾

Mother-Cat

Heather Cameron

She is silent in her approach but I know she is there, as she pushes her nose against the door. It is the cold time of the morning, just before dawn and, from within my burrowed-warmth, I can see the misting rain settling on the greyness outside. She sits now at the end of my bed, calmly licking the silver fine droplets from her fur. I watch her. I hold out my hand, and her steady green gaze flicks across me. She delicately steps her way across my bed and settles within reach of my hand. I recognise the privilege I am being given and pat her gently. I am rewarded with a growing scratchy hum that vibrates her whiskers and the fur beneath her mouth. I smile at her and her eyes close into a cat smile.

I lie on my side in this bed, my knees drawn up, my arms around the pillow. She curls into the empty semi-circle my body has made. Her back and shoulders are rounded and her fur is close to my face, small bits of it move with my breath. I smell her cat smell; it is warmth and pine-needle crispness and soft rain combined. I run my hand across her softness between the ears, down the back. She turns inside out, her head upside down and stretches all four legs at once. She becomes a perfect circle. I mirror her movement and we lie, our heads beside each others, our necks twisted, our eyes to the ceiling. Her purr has slowed and is a whisper. Her eyes close. I untwist my neck and the pitch of her humming rises. We both settle, her cheek resting on her paws, nose buried in her tail. My cheek rests on the pillow, and I remember…

I am a child, young and clumsy with the cold, but I am wise enough to know I am watching an ancient ritual. I am engrossed in the beauty of this cat, speckled with grain colour on black fur. Her smooth sleekness has been plump now for several weeks and we have found her in the shoe cupboard, the linen drawer and in my bed. My mother has known and spoken warnings that my father seemed not to hear. My sister has chattered excitedly at school about the kittens. My brother has questioned the how, why and when, but he has, as usual, been ignored. I have been silent. I have stroked her sleekness and stared into her amber eyes. And now I sit in a silent vigil beside this warm nest of hay in the shed and I watch her as she works hard to lick clean each new body that gushes from her body. She purrs and whispers to them, as they seek out her nipples. Their minute paws push in rhythm against her body as they suck. I know that I am crying as I watch their blind noisy fumbling and she smiles her cat smile at me.

It is night and from my bed I can see the stars growing brighter in the blackness outside my window. It is a cold night, but my body is colder. It feels a coldness that cannot be warmed. I hear the mother cat miaowing as she paces the ground outside. I hear the rustling as she moves through the flower garden. I hear the emptiness in her call, and its echo jumps and flickers in my body. While I ate lunch today, my father went to the shed and took the kittens from their mother. He placed them in an old paint can, filled it with water, put the lid on the can, and placed a red brick on top of it. The can sits at the door of the shed.

I have sat in the garden this afternoon and watched the mother cat walk in circles, her soft paws urgent, her voice desperate in its calling. I do not know how to stop crying. My mother has told me to stop being silly, that we have to be sensible, that I am upsetting my father. 'He does not like having to do these things, but they've got to be done.' I look at my father but his face has not changed. He is not changed. He does not look at me.

The cat jumps from the garden up onto my window-sill. She is silent, knowing that I have heard her. I watch my bedroom door as I slowly get out of the bed and open the window. She leaps through the opening, onto my bed, and together we burrow down into the blankets. She does not call anymore, and I am silent too. I hold her curled within my arms, but she does not purr. She licks the wetness from my cheek with her sandpaper tongue, and I bury my face in her fur. I wish with all my young-old heart that I could do something to change this day, but I cannot. We lie, this cat and child-I, in my bed, and the stars come and go silently in the night sky.

Heather Cameron *lives on the Surf Coast, Victoria, with her partner, two sons and one wild cat named Charlie. She has had a life-long affinity with cats, and was probably a cat in a previous life. She has had the privilege of being in loving relationships with many special cats, and has gained much wisdom from them, especially on how to eat rich foods, sleep in luxurious places, and get as much patting and loving as possible.*

Section Five CATacombs

Familiar

Bridget Musters

for Merlin

Night closes round us
you in your corner, I in mine
concentrated in a single pool of light
fat furry moths plick the black square of the window pane
you are oblivious, suddenly old.

When we were young you fitted my new-married hand.
Later you alone heard verbal torrents
watched me hurled across the room
until we fled across the world.

For sixteen years you've been my shadow
most constant companion of the sheets
but now no longer like a Christmas stocking in the dark
do you anchor the duvet against the draught
inhibit intimacy
wake me when it's time you think to eat.

Last week you thundered down the hall
perforated thighs with claws too old to sheathe
waited at the bathroom door
the bedroom door, the garden path
brought rats lined parallel for my inspection.
Last week you left your footprints on the page.

This week you walk stiffly—when at all
eat nothing, sleep in a hidden corner
stare into space, grey silk and bone.

I've rehearsed for years the separation of the ways
for pain is after all an old and easy feeling
familiar
but the how and when are not my choosing.
Cats whisper in Tibetan poets' ears
I do not think you'll speak again to me.

Bridget Musters *has always had cats in her life, and Merlin was particularly special. She had her from a kitten, and took her when she emigrated from the UK to New Zealand, where she now lives in Nelson. She's a writer of poetry and short stories, which have won several awards, and is currently working on a novel.*

Cats Do Go to Heaven

Cath McNaughton

for Mary O'Brien (8 July 1926–17 October 1998)

Over the forty-four years Mary and I lived together, there have been nine cats, nine lives. Seven of these lives we nurtured together. Of the other two, one was Mary's childhood cat, Pokey by name, a handsome black tom. In spite of rationing during the war years, Mary saw that he had his share of raw fish. The other one is Alice who came to me after Mary died and is still around.

Our first cat together was Lucretia, a roman cat, not a borgia—black-and-white—and small enough to nestle in Mary's dressing gown pocket. She could be fierce and came from a long line of independent, almost wild cats, from Bout de l'Lisle at the extreme end of Montréal Island. Cretia lived for fourteen years and died in Toronto not long after we moved here. A diet of 'Puss in Boots' and raw liver seemed to predispose her to kidney disease.

Mary and I were bereft after her death vowing that, in due course, we would adopt two cats, so as never to be looking over our shoulders for the cat that wasn't there. And so Ms and Xanthippe entered our lives. Xanthippe or Xippe as she was known, was a brown tabby, slightly handicapped and a real nag for food.

Her handicap was caused by a long imprisonment in a cage, much too small for her; she never recovered her coordination. Xippe was maternal with Ms, a shy, slight white-and-brown cat much beloved by Mary. Travelling out west and camping, we took the cats with us but sadly Ms was killed in Regina when she became frightened by a sudden noise and ran out of the camper on to the Trans Canada highway.

Back in Toronto, Xippe seemed a bit lonesome and some neighbourhood kids brought us MacGonigle, a delightful silver-grey kitten. As he grew, we found that he was really a grey tabby with elegant silver stripes. He was extremely affectionate with charming manners and we learned that he daily called on the seniors' residence nearby, as well as many of our neighbours. Alas, our experience with little male cats has not been a happy one. Even when neutered they tend to wander off and so we lost MacGonigle and later a gorgeous ginger fellow named Hamish.

Xippe had, of course, reared both kittens and so we had to find another mate. About that time, Mary decided that cats needed more respect and should have two names. Rather than give them our names, we settled on well loved fictional characters. Maggie

Tulliver was the runt of a litter, a tiny brown tabby with a huge personality. She attached herself firmly to me, while Xippe, noisily demanding more and more food, could always get Mary to open the fridge.

One day we found a small mole-like area on Xippe's face and when investigated, it was found to be malignant. It seemed so unfair that this dear ungainly mama cat could not be allowed to live to a comfortable old age. All we could do was give her a lovely big meal and then Mary took her on her last journey to the vet.

Several months later, when we had both decided that Maggie Tulliver was getting unbearably bossy, we acquired Morag Gunn. Morag was almost the perfect cat: quiet, affectionate, and not greedy. During Mary's illness they were always together. The comfort Morag gave seemed beyond human touch. In these difficult days, both cats became ill. Maggie to succumb to kidney failure and Morag diagnosed with diabetes. However it was possible to treat her and she survived for six months after Mary died. Morag's death was like a cataclysm to me—like the end of an era.

Friends advised me to have a dog but there was a waiting period, the house was quiet and I was so used to cats.

So enter Alice, a pretty, extremely, agile, brown-and-white tabby. Living outside she had a sad history of losing her litter to a raccoon. Fortunately, the humane society found her and gave her to me, speyed and protected. She appears to like living here although I would like her to stand up more to Vickie who is a pushy Bichon. I find that a cat is usually too intelligent to learn from a human being. So for all my urgings, Alice tolerates a good deal of robust canine play.

The nine felines in our lives were pretty important to us, from Lucretia in 1960 to Morag in 1999—almost forty years of joint cats. We really came to know each other through these animals. They amused us, distracted us as they always had to be fed. They rubbed our legs when they sensed a disagreement and curled up beside

us to show we belonged to them. At seventy-four, I'm glad I still have Alice—cats surely are a gift to women.

Cath McNaughton met Mary O'Brien almost fifty years ago in Glasgow, Scotland. As midwives in their first job they became friends and feminists. Mary went on to graduate teaching and to write the Politics of Reproduction. *Their partnership with each other and their cats was to last through illnesses, career changes and through the long painful journey that is Alzheimer's disease.* 🐾

After

Maika Greene

After

After the abortion mostly my baby goes into the sky, into the sunset clouds out my window. Me lying in bed sad unbelieving, clouds moving away too quickly. But some of the baby goes into my cat and I love her with a new depth. We dance together to Peggy Lee. She likes that.

Before

I come back from Queensland, two weeks holiday. She is not happy to see me. She has been getting along with catsitter boy much too well. She walks away from me towards him, curls her tail to brush his shoulder, he whispers her name, she purrs. He has taken beautiful photos of her, but he never lets me have copies. He stays the night. I sleep beside them.

After

I make her a website. She doesn't care. The only photo I have is of her neck, too close as she got bored of posing for me, got up, walked away.

Factory cat poor factory cat no trees no long grass. I take her to the country, I want her to see the bush. Now you can be a bush cat I say. She is excited. She strolls under a caravan, wants to inspect that exciting long piece of metal, smell it good and hard, delicately and painstakingly. Doesn't care about trees. Much interest in what people store under caravans. No bush cat here, nosey gossip cat instead. I wait beside the other people's caravan for almost an hour.

In summer she lies in the sun knocks herself out so much sometimes I wonder if she is dead.

Sometimes she is too lazy even to close her eyes, lies there sleeping with them open. Disorientated and wobbly as she comes too.

In winter she sits close to the heater closer closer and closer she always gets the best spot. The first time she burns her fur I don't know what that smell is and neither does she. She looks up around sniff sniff. Every winter we try a new heater but every year holes in the fur on her sides. I write about the heater fights. I can't even answer the phone without bringing her because she will sneak too close again. She thinks I am mean, denying her her Heater God.

She is a happy cat. Sometimes just the fact that the sun is rising makes her purr so loudly you can hear her washing herself in the other room, walking down the hall. Sometimes she runs jumps into bed lies beside me purr purr purr and I lie there too very awake now but worth it.

Before

I wrote: I can never give up the idea that there must be something. And mostly then I hug my cat and it is her and me. But sometimes I don't love my cat and there is only bored eternal blankness.

Sometimes happens less often After.

After

The brain tumor makes her grumpy. She stamps louder than you'd think a cat could. She paces, she tramples on my head while I sleep, I am covered in scratches. I write about her claws. I take her to vets and vets until I know the vet-stress

is too much for her and they don't do any good, even the Chinese medicine one. When the fits start they give me cortisone tables to give her and her 'quality of life' comes good. She is not blind anymore even. She has irritable bowel and the only food she can eat is cooked chicken. The only food she *will* eat is Bi-lo's barbequed chicken. She won't touch barbequed chicken from Coles or from the chicken shop down the street. She gets very fat.

The last fit doesn't stop. I hold her paw while they give her the injection I see the peace come into her eyes. Back at home before that strange sounds, so strange I can barely believe they are coming from my mouth. Bruises on my hand from hitting the wall. My brain feeling squashed inside from both sides. Trying so hard to make everything seem real again. I want to say goodbye but she never regains enough consciousness. I drive up past Geelong late the next day and get her cremated. Recognise the smell of her burning fur.

After After

I think I hear her in the next room, at the end of my bed. I hear the sounds of her walking but she's not there and I wonder if it was ever really the sound of her walking at all. Ten years together just her and me it's a long time. Fourteen years alive it's not bad. She comes to me in dreams. She tramples on my head. I hold her up to drink water. I don't know what to do with her bowls.

Lia and **Maika Greene** *lived together for ten years. The last three were in a factory in inner city Melbourne. Maika got Lia when she first moved out of home, at seventeen. Lia was four and in need of a new owner. They used to go on holidays to the country together. Maika works as a youth worker and does creative writing. Lia died on 28 October 2002.* 🐾

Artistry Terry Wolverton

1. 1978

Color bleeds from her dissolving house—pink
kitchen molten, green living room fluxed; gold
ring joins the first one, discarded in dark
drawer. Bed shorn of comfort leeches white.

New apartment drab, suburban. Eggshell
walls, gray spectrum of TV. Carport. Trash
compactor. Black telephone. Forty-six,
the first time in her life she's lived alone.

Her only daughter—hair glows henna
under California sun—exhorts
her to take up the palette, paint fissured
walls of her life in brilliant chroma.

But after work, silent rooms drain pigment,
render nights long, bleached bone, ashen as ghosts.

2. 2000

One morning the old cat leaves, hobbles on
spindled legs into eternity. Takes
with her the puling cries for tuna, hairs
that carpeted my black sweaters, steady
gaze of her topaz eyes. I'm forty-five;
two rings abandoned in a velvet box.
When the key turns and my door swings open,
dark silence greets me like the breath of god.

When my mother married for the third time,
I sneered and sent no presents, sure she'd failed
to grasp the art of solitude. Now TV
flickers blue against my sinking face;
as inspiration falters, pigments reek,
the brush has grown near weightless in my hand.

Terry Wolverton *is the author of*
Insurgent Muse: Life and Art at
the Woman's Building, *a memoir;
and* Bailey's Beads, *a novel.
A novel-in-poems,* Embers,
is forthcoming in 2003.

Pusscat Darling

Jo Stavros

Relationships were changing. Moving in was the next step, and apparently I wasn't the only one thinking this was a good place to be. She was a stray. Small, black and scrawny. A good mouse catcher. She was such a good mouse catcher that bowls of food followed. We were impressed. This was considered a serious move, as we were both quite shy of commitment and responsibility, which included caring for a cat. For a time we considered her a visitor, not ours. So she remained nameless for the thirteen years she stayed with us. Friends referred to her as my 'baby'. No way, she was no 'baby'. She could look after herself. She was always my mate, my Pusscat Darling.

We moved house, and then moved again. This time a house with a backyard. Pusscat loved the garden. We kept each other company. I would dig the garden bed and she, unable to resist such an offering, would rework it later. She had her favourite plants, some she ate, some she slept under and others she battled. We repeated this routine, working and lazing about in the sun for years. Her dark shadow of a presence always about. Then she disappeared. And not just for a couple of days.

As the days passed, I thought about what might have happened. People contributed their own not-so-hopeful or helpful thoughts. Poisoned! Caught in a bag and battered by someone hating cats! What were these people thinking? Morbid thoughts fuelled my already panicked imagination. Had she been attacked or mauled by a dog? Was she trapped in someone's shed, starving? Had she been hit by a car and now lay wounded under someone else's house? No comfort from my thoughts either.

We distributed notices in letterboxes, placed ads in the newspaper lost and found, and visited cat shelters. Try it. Walk into a cat shelter and see all those caged cats, but not yours, turn towards you—with eyes imploring. This at the time seemed incredibly sad, too sad. The decision was made, a turning point. There was no reason to torture myself further. There was no longer any desire to indulge in nightmare scenarios. There was enough heartache with her missing.

As the weeks passed, my garden began to show signs of neglect. No more nurturing. The garden became a reminder for my little loneliness. My love for gardening was very much tied up with her company. This connection surprised me. Pusscat's presence lingered. Her always asleep in the shadows. The sound of her paws on the floorboards. A momentary hope followed by disappointment. There was a haunting. And then there was an acceptance of loss. I chose the least painful explanation for Pusscat's disappearance. She had begun to lose teeth, and had become quite grey. She was old. Maybe ill. The emotional need for resolution. Go gently, rest in peace.

Seven weeks later. She's at the window wanting to be let in. I get the phone call at work. Disbelief. My heart remembers its ache. I want to rush home and hold her again. She is skinny and in need of care. However, she has a perfectly round, smooth patch on her head. No fur, no wound, no scar. Very odd. We take her to the vet. No ideas there. Friends ask where was she was all this time. I question Pusscat, searching for clues. She looks back at me. Silence. I tell them that no matter how much I ask, she just won't tell me.

One explanation not considered before and now jokingly bandied about—alien abduction. Decide it is as plausible as the others are. The heart mends, but the joy is tinged with warning of future sadness. It is hard to dispel the inevitable. Pusscat Darling became very affectionate. Her feisty temperament mellowed. We had one more year together. My darling Pusscat.

Jo Stavros lives in Melbourne. She works part time in the disability area, studies part time, remains in a full-time relationship. She enjoys gardening again, mostly on account of the feline companionship.

Deaf Eurydice

Suniti Namjoshi

For Suki (d. 27 July 1997)

Sometimes the murmur of longing is so
tentative, and the thought of a caress so
tangential, that the senses strain to hear what,
after all, cannot be said.

                                  And it's then that
the temptation arises: to write a lie
on the water, scribblings on sand, or to descry
from the way the leaves moved and the light
fell what shadows portend. This is twilight
time, Orpheus time, Demeter time, when they
call the long dead, and deaf Eurydice
struggles to hear and hearing nothing falls behind
till her footfall makes no imprint save on the mind.

*Suniti Namjoshi's books include
St Suniti and the Dragon;
Building Babel and Goja. Suki
was a lilac Burmese (1984-1997).
She was much loved and very
loving. She died of diabetes.*

Kari Kerry Greenwood

When I first met her she fitted into the palm of my hand.

The children in the street had found her, four weeks old, soaking wet, staggering along the gutter. Sole survivor of a massacre. I took her into my hands. Tabby and white. Eyes just open on a cold, hungry universe stared into mine. Her little tail was a perfect triangle. Wobbly but not defeated. She opened her tiny pink mouth and mewed and I was lost.

My dearest friend David and I fed her sweet, diluted milk and wore her next to our skin so that she should not take cold. I used to stick her down my front, between my breasts, where there is a suitable gully and she would snuggle down and sleep, never scratching. She was a little purring island of glowing warmth. David called her Kari after Kari Solmundasen in Njal's Saga, the only survivor of the murder of Njal and his household. The name made her strong.

When she waded into a senior cat's food with squeaks of joy it was a relief to us all (except poor Bootle, who was affronted. He did not like kittens in his Fishy Dins).

She was the only cat I ever knew who liked cars. She travelled with David when he drove me to work and as she got bigger, she scaled him and sat on his shoulder as if she had just dislodged the parrot. When the car broke down on the way home once, David walked through Footscray in his pjs with a cat on his shoulder. No one was surprised. Wizards can get away with anything.

When I started to write novels, Kari sat with me. She would leap onto the desk, find a corner, and gradually slump from alert-cat-on-guard to sleepy-cat-with-folded-paws, then would wake, shake herself, and go back to an imitation of the statue of Basht. If I had been sitting too long, she would place one paw very gently on the keyboard and suggest that it was time to get up, stretch, and make a cup of coffee (me) and a saucer of milk (Kari). When I was sick, she would lie on my chest and wash my face with her small rough tongue.

She loved tucking herself into small spaces. Opening a drawer was fraught with surprise when I was likely to find it full of fur, not the underwear I had expected. I took to leaving spaces in bookshelves into which she would fit herself, surrounded by dark volumes which contrasted beautifully with the tabby-and-white coat. She would sprawl across a newspaper, covering a surprising amount of news, so that it could only be read by moving the cat gradually off the interesting article.

And she stayed with me all through the nights when I wrote and wrote and the house was dark and the world was silent and nothing stirred except the busy fingers on the keyboard and the clack of the printer and the occasionally wide, toothy yawn of a cat who was terribly sleepy but would not allow herself to fall into slumber while there was work to be done.

Then she got old. I gave her Pentavite to pep up her system and an old rabbit fur coat to snuggle into when it got cold. Every winter I dreaded the coming of the deep cold, thinking I might lose her. She grew fragile and grumpy and rickety but her spirit never failed. I found her a fluffy blanket which trapped heat and she stayed. She stayed with me for seventeen years.

And when she died she died like a human, with grace and acceptance and, as I had when she was a kitten, I carried her in my arms for two days as she gradually allowed death to creep over her. She was not assaulted or violated by death. She was just allowing death to take her, slowly, as my own grandmother had died, sinking into death as she had snuggled into the warmth of a quilt. At first she clung to me, but after the first night her grip grew weaker and finally she relinquished her hold on life and died as gently and quietly as a falling leaf. I only knew that she was dead when her body grew cold. Seventeen years of my life died with her.

I buried her in my garden. I will never forget her.

Kerry Greenwood has written twenty six novels and has worked as folk-singer, factory hand, director, producer, editor, translator, costume-maker, cook, and qualified as a solicitor. She is an honorary Greek. She is a historian. She works part-time for Victoria Legal Aid as an advocate in Magistrates' Courts and is currently working on her thirteenth Phryne Fisher book. She has written four science fiction novels for young adults and is also writing in the Crime Wave series The Three Pronged Dagger *(which won a Davitt Award for juvenile crime fiction)* The Wandering Icon *and the upcoming* Danger: Do Not Enter.

She is not married, has no children and lives with three cats Monsieur, Aise and Belladonna and an accredited Wizard.

Misty-eyed

Margaret Fearn

I've had many cats over the years and loved them all, but Misty was the only one who turned my heart to marshmallow—she had that x factor.

There was just something about her that totally ensnared me. She had a mystique all of her own.

My young son and I often paid a visit to the local pet shop where we would look at the fish, birds and animals offered for sale. One particular day, we spied three adorable bundles of grey fluff curled-up, asleep. Two had already been sold but the available one opened her eyes and came to the side of the cage to be stroked—we were hooked!

Driving home I worried what my husband was going to say because we already had two cats, a canary and several goldfish. I needn't have, for this little fur-ball had the knack of winning anyone over with one glance—a 'femme fatale' if ever I saw one! Every time I looked at her I swear I felt my heart lurch. She was just so adorable.

It was a misty day when we bought her and this, coupled with her soft grey coat, made the name Misty seem appropriate. But her sweet looks were deceiving. She was the naughtiest, most conniving creature and, within a week, her name had been changed to Mitz the bitch. 'Misty' was too mellow for this bundle of dynamite!

Her favorite trick was to dive-bomb me each morning as I walked through the kitchen door and climb up my pyjama legs, or up my back while I was talking on the phone. As a consequence, I was always covered in scratches and little puncture marks.

Hanging washing on the line came to be a battle of wits—I'd try to peg the clothes and she would take a flying leap and swing on underwear, sheets or towels. She tried them all. I'm sure she had monkey genes in her!

A favorite sleeping spot was on top of the microwave or on my slippers, especially if I was wearing them. Some evenings she would curl up on my knee and be so loving that I couldn't believe she was the same creature. She reminded me of my children. When I looked at their angelic sleeping faces I forgave all their naughtiness and felt love overwhelm me.

Somehow this little feline had surpassed the emotion I felt for my other pets and lodged in a special niche that only she could fill. It didn't matter how destructive or mischievous she was, one meow and a beseeching look for a cuddle would have me scooping her up and murmuring the most absurd endearments to her.

I was to visit relations in Christchurch for a few days while my husband was to be chief cook and child/pet minder at home. 'Don't worry, we'll be fine,' were his parting words when I voiced my anxiety. Ringing mid-week I was reassured that everything was under control. But as soon as I alighted from the plane and saw my son's miserable face, I knew something was wrong.

'It's Misty,' he sobbed. 'She's dead!' Apparently she had been found bleeding in the back yard and we still don't know what happened. I was devastated.

No other animal had ever been able to claim such a large piece of my heart. It has taken me a long time to finish grieving. Misty will be a part of me forever.

Margaret Fearn *lives in Nelson, a beautiful part of New Zealand. She's interested in gardening, writing, art and old sailing ships. With children, grandchildren and many friends she considers herself very fortunate.*

Annapurna's Absence

Martha Davidson

Annapurna was not my first cat. I'd grown up in a household filled with cats —sometimes three or four at a time—and I'd had one cat of my own before her: Grendel, who'd died in kittenhood, hit by a taxi. But since Annapurna's reign in the 1970s and '80s, I've never had another. I say it is because I don't want the burden or responsibility of feedings and kitty litter, the guilt of abandoning an animal when I am away. But the truth may be that she still occupies too large a place in my heart to let another cat in. Annapurna filled my life with affection and amusement. I still miss her.

She was a half-sibling of Grendel the huntress, whose short life had ended tragically as she dashed back across the street to show me a prize worm she'd snared in a neighbour's garden. Annapurna was not a huntress, though she knew how to track a bug or stalk a pigeon. Her area of expertise was sun basking, belly up. And what a belly it was! Large and very furry, it could be—and sometimes was—mistaken for a small rug. Spread-eagled on her back, she somehow managed to follow the sun's course from window to window throughout the day. Unlike many furry creatures, she welcomed belly rubs.

Annapurna was part tabby-part Maine coon cat. Her face was tiger-ish, her fur long, and her body perhaps disproportionately large (when she reached twelve pounds, the vet put her on a diet). Her tail was plume-like and magnificent. She could not meow. My upstairs neighbour, Peter, had tried in vain to give her voice lessons when she was a kitten. It was several years before I found out that she had been born with paralysed vocal cords. She could purr, however, though as she got older purring, too, became difficult for her, and she would have to pull away from petting sessions until she could calm down and catch her breath.

She was good company. I worked at home as a freelance researcher and writer, and taking breaks to rub her belly or look out the window with her was a good way to reduce stress and focus on the important things in life. Purna (as I often called her) saw me through two apartments in Cambridge, Massachusetts, through several boyfriends and periods of boyfriendlessness, and through the ups and downs of freelancing. I saw her through the birth of her kittens, motherhood, minor afflictions, and old age. She was popular with all my friends and beloved by some of them.

When I think of her now, nearly twenty years later, what I remember most clearly are our times of separation. The first occurred when she was about a year old. For reasons I no longer remember—perhaps her spaying—she was on a medication that must have made her confused or disoriented. An indoor cat, she managed to get out and wander away. She did not turn up when I searched the neighbourhood for her, calling her name. A day or two went by, and recalling Grendel's death, I imagined the worst, but a friend persuaded me to put up handbills around the neighbourhood. I drew a sketch of Annapurna with my phone number and the caption 'Large cat lost. Reward for return.' A few more days went by, and my hope faded. Then one evening the doorbell rang, and outside were a young man and woman holding Annapurna. They had seen the poster, and when they spotted Annapurna several blocks away, they immediately guessed she was the large lost cat. The tag on her collar, with my phone number and address, confirmed it. They refused the reward: they had lost a pet once, they told me, that someone had returned to them, and they were happy they could bring me the same kind of joy as they had been given.

Our other separations were caused by my wanderings, not hers. In 1976 I had an opportunity to travel with the English rock group Jethro Tull as their tea lady (a sort of caterer and chauffeur) on a six-week tour of the Midwest and Canada. The person who was subletting my apartment did not want to care for my cat, so Annapurna went to stay with my parents in the suburbs of New York. In the airports, hotels, stadiums and concert halls that formed my world for a month and a half, I often missed that furry belly. I picked her up on my way back to Boston and we flew home together—Purna stuffed into a too-small pet carrier under my seat in the plane, both of us intensely anxious for her liberation when we were safely home again.

Our next parting was nearly ten years later, when I got a grant to study photo collections in South America. It would entail a three-month trip, and my friend Sue, whose own cat had died not long before, offered to take care of Purna in her New York apartment while I was away. My sister picked us up in Cambridge and drove us to Manhattan. Purna had been sedated for the trip, and by the time we reached the city, the medication had caused severe diarrhoea. It was an ignominious entrance to Purna's New York experience, and I was sure that Sue was regretting her offer. But Sue was big-hearted and forgiving, and Annapurna, it turned out, was able to repay Sue's kindness by helping her win a photo contest. A series of slides that Sue took of Annapurna as she tried to stalk a squirrel through Sue's apartment window won a top prize at a 'slide night' gathering. And only years afterwards did I learn that a large hole in the arm of Sue's black leather recliner was the work of a certain cat.

When Annapurna and I were finally reunited in Cambridge after that trip, she ignored me for most of a day. It was proper punishment for my abandoning her, and it made me reconsider my plans for her when I would leave again later that year to continue my research in Mexico. Purna had aged noticeably in those three months, or perhaps I was just seeing her more clearly after her absence. She was thinner (perhaps a good thing) and had more difficulty breathing, her vocal cords apparently blocking the passage of air. It saddened me to see her halt an activity or pull away from a good bout of petting in her struggle to breathe. I did not want to leave her again.

So our final separation was pre-arranged before my next trip, by appointment with a compassionate veterinarian who made house calls to euthanase pets. A former roommate who was a woodworker built a special mahogany box and, although I knew animals were best buried directly in the ground, it was consoling to think of her in such a secure shelter. My landlord's son dug a hole in the back yard, and my friend Camilla came to be with us when the vet arrived. Annapurna was napping at the top of the stairs. We slipped newspaper under her, and the vet gave the injection. Within seconds, it seemed, Purna was gone, her eyes without light, her body light as feathers. That evening I put together an album of photos of her, and I looked at it frequently in the days before I left.

A few weeks later, on a bus in Mexico on the Day of the Dead, I looked out the window and saw, on the side of the road near a woman with a bundle of marigolds, a cat that looked very much like Annapurna. I was comforted.

Martha Davidson is a freelance picture researcher and writer now living in Washington, DC. She does not have a pet, but enjoys the visits of feline neighbours and the companionship of a man who claims to be a cat.

Casting Spells for Cats

Lesley Fowler

Born in an incinerator

Lirry and Shasta were born in K's incinerator and we only knew they were there when they staggered, malnourished and confused, out into the garden, lurching amongst the ti-tree and grevillea saplings, dwarfed by their tiny stems. They were the offspring of the neighbour's cat who had been kicked and unfed for most of her life.

When we discovered the kittens, K went next door, told off the neighbours, told them they didn't deserve to have a cat, and that from now on the mother and kittens were hers.

Brittle with despair

There were three kittens. K kept the strongest. I couldn't condemn either of the weak ones to the possibility of an early death and took them both: they'd be company for each other when I was out, I thought, and they were, sitting side by identical side at the end of the driveway receiving compliments from passers-by and lying with their brotherly arms around each other's necks in front of the fire in the winter.

It took six months before they decided to live. During that time I ran one or other of them to the vet about once a fortnight with a string of ailments. Shasta was worse. His black fur was dry and brittle with despair and his body was rigid with terror. I spent a lot of time stroking and cuddling them both and I put in extra time with him. He'd lie on my lap stiff as a metal cast of himself. His fur looked and felt like a wire scouring pad. He'd let me pick him up, put him on my lap and would lie there until I put him down. My hand went over and over him, the scratchy fur bending under my hand, his body unyielding.

Flaming Beauty and The Essence of Being

Their names had to be right. Words are powerful. The right name makes a difference.

I gave Lirry a name derived from the Chinese hexagram Li, which means Flaming Beauty. Despite the illnesses and the rocky start to his life, he had an inner light. Even now, in his seventeenth year, he is still incandescent. I asked a friend, a Sanskrit scholar, to tell me about Sanskrit words that meant 'being able to live at peace with yourself, in your own skin'. I wanted a word that would give my rigid cat life. 'Svasti' she said, and my tongue turned it into Shasta. I never thought of the daisy, though that's what most people thought he was named for. Each time I called him, his name brought him to his true self.

In the kitchen

My kitchen is an oblong room and my house is old enough for the kitchen to be big, a room you live in. I often sit in a chair by the window and work or read or talk to friends. I was sitting there with Shasta in my lap, brushing him. He was as rigid as ever in one moment and in the next he relaxed. His entire body softened. Later that day he began to shed his wire coat; he grew a silky new coat in a couple of weeks.

Lilac and cotoneaster

Lirry and Shasta had different routes up to the roof. Lirry took to a sloping branch of lilac which ran alongside the carport; you'd see his black-and-white flashing in and out of the green and lilac as he made his way up. From the fairly flat-topped carport, he'd jump to the pitched roof of the house. Shasta went up by the cotoneaster at the back end of the carport. Arrived, they'd sling their long, black, shining bodies on the chimney top or on a sheltered slope of the roof and lope down when I drove in. One day Shasta stayed on the carport roof. He walked up and down, miaowing when he reached the end which faced the back garden, where I stood, not far from the cotoneaster.

'Beautiful Shasta,' I told him. 'Lovely cat. Come on down.' He turned his back on me and walked to the other end of the roof, turned, approached me again, miaowed. Once more he came to the edge, looked down at me, calling fiercely, and then backed off. Again and again.

sta the bold, the brave the beautiful

Beloved Linny

I got the ladder out, climbed up and brought him down.

Chaos coming

A tumour was pressing on his spine. He was easily disoriented though most of the time he stayed close to me. I took him under the covers at night and he snuggled up and purred against my skin. Lirry luxuriated in the extra space on top of the bed. I kept Shas inside while I was at work, and one day came home to a house in chaos. He had emptied his body out in every way and in every place. He was pushed up against the kitchen wall, trying to get through it. His claws were out and his toes splayed wide. I held him and didn't let go till he died.

A neat shelf

K came round the next day to help me dig his grave. We took turns on the pick at first but she is much stronger and more skilful at such work and did most of it.

I'd chosen a fairly unvegetated patch along the fence opposite my bedroom window, a spot Shas had favoured if he'd been out at night. After a few hours' illicit hunting he'd wait patiently there for dawn when I'd open the curtains. Up he'd get then and trot round to the door for his first legitimate meal.

I spent a lot time leaning on the shovel while K dug, wanting some greater moment for the occasion, something to match my grief, but unable to work out what it might be. Organ music might have done. Or Tibetan thigh-bone trumpets and drums. K distracted me with the story of interring the ashes of a friend whose body had been cremated overseas, the bones not ground down to the fineness we're used to here. Identifiable shards of bone had slid out of the urn.

She finished work on the grave and I took up the wrapped bundle of Shasta's body and knelt down.

He didn't fit. One of his legs stuck stiffly out. I remembered a doco I'd seen in which some mortuary assistants talked about having had to break the legs of a (human) body to extricate it from the position into which he'd rigidified. I held Shassy's body close. K hadn't seen the doco. '*I* know,' she said and, swinging the pick side-on, dug a neat shelf for his leg.

__Lesley Fowler__ lives in Canberra where she writes poetry, fiction and non-fiction which has been widely published and broadcast. Her first collection of poetry was Crossing the Sky, *(Five Islands Press). She has also published a collection of short fiction* Washing My Mother's Hair.

Section Six AristoCATs

Velvet Prince

Marge Piercy

The velvet prince, you slept always
pressed to my side
in the bed where you were born.

You would lie with your mother,
lover, playmate, a pillow or grey
fur with four sharp perked ears.

Gentleman, lover, inheriting
top cat position in middle age
and never losing a fight because

you never fought but intimidated,
puffing yourself like a blowfish,
uttering threats that froze the blood

protecting your females who adored
you. Even at the end when you could
scarcely lift your head, they

washed you, kept you warm.
I wake in the mornings without your
purring as I sip my cappuchino

rising to the day through the skim
of sleep like boiled milk over me
and the day is empty of you.

I have loved my familiars all my life.
You were my soul wrapped in fur.
The lack of you lessens me.

Marge Piercy is the author of sixteen collections of poetry including What are Big Girls Made Of?, The Art of Blessing the Day: Poems with a Jewish Theme *and* Colors Passing Through Us, *all from Knopf. Her most recent novel* The Third Child *will come out this November. In 2001, Leapfrog Press brought out* So You Want to Write: How To Master the Craft of Writing Fiction and the Personal Narrative, *co-authored with Ira Wood. Her memoir,* Sleeping with Cats, *was published by HarperCollins.*

The Luxury of Cats

Cathy Saba

My name is CAThy, but in truth, I'm CATherine. My beloved grandmother referred to me as 'CATtarina', whether in her firmest tone or in the loving airiness that was her eager voice seeking me out. I close my eyes in wonderful reminiscence and reflect upon being her favourite *Cattarina*. In the here and now, solely the tapping of select fingers, letter by letter, my un-choreographed chorus line of keyboard. I type away, in the wretched reluctance of knowing full well that in this lifetime I will never hear *'Cattarina'* again.

The greatest pose for a painter's canvas is the posse on my couch, on a grey and wintry day. Tiger is a lightweight and melts down waxed on my rib cage. Alley is hefty and often warms my aching pelvis. Mickey, in her wisdom and graciousness, curls at my feet like a live bookend. We purr together tremendously, as a post-modern symphony orchestra might, deliciously untimed, undefined, and yet staged together. I feel a Cheshire-cat-like smile busting out of my gaze, in a soft fluidity it expands to meet the heart-felt warmth within me and caramelises into glorious contentment and catnapping chemistry.

Ah… 'tis the language of cats that stirred my earliest child-like intrigue. Sometimes in mere myriads of mellowness, and at other times in the sincerest need, *feed me, stroke me, see me, play with me, tune in to me, know ME*—and, well, yes—I did. I was an only child and I do remember feeling some of those all too familiar pangs. Alas they miaow, *miaow*, miaow, in their sensual and pleasing individuality, yet blending in precision to any tongue; English, Italian, Spanish—maybe even French, it matters not. Instinctively they know no such boundaries, because cat-speak is truly infinite with tone. I am in awe of Tiger's brazened attitude and her sphinx-like posture that delivers her high self-esteem. I am comforted by Alley's bulging stretched out belly; this vulnerability denotes a trust in me. I am forgiven by Mickey's atomic purr and clad-curling-motion paws making their souvenir tracks in my lap. This means I am still loved despite and, in between, Tiger and Alley's frequent and competitive barrages ahead of her, in approaches for my affection. So doest speak the language of cats.

I love cat sayings, poetic cat tales and the like. And wisdom does exist herein. My fridge magnet reads *the more I know about men, the more I love my cats*. Well I guess I'll love my cats to death, but that is true of me anyway. So lo and behold this is not a CATastrophy, it is a conscious choice.

The Bengal, the Siberian, tigers; these are the wildcats I find the most severely intoxicating. Yet captured so alluringly, amongst all the beautiful species, in a book photographically and poetically dedicated to all cats great and small, is *Vavra's Cats*. And at home I am agreeable with Wanda Toscanini Horowitz who quotes *I love cats because they are so beautiful aesthetically. They are like sculpture walking around the house.* In my heart I tell myself the same as Theophile Gautier did in that *who can believe that there is no soul behind those luminous eyes.*

When I was a child I watched a beautiful relationship unveil in a film called 'Where the North Wind Blows'. For some time now I have vowed I will search it out to revisit the magic betwixt one man and tiger cubs that grew up with him. To myself I say, Cathy if you wanted a relationship with wild beasts such as tigers you should have been a vet and applied at the zoo. Nevertheless, one day in my travels, I will hold a cub in my very own hands. I think of this as a living wish that disturbingly seems to be more sacred than the actual fantasies and desires I have of some human beings. Oh well, you could very well say, the cat is out of the bag!

Cathy is completing a post graduate diploma of psychology at Ballarat University. In her spare time Cathy enjoys painting on silk, nature walks with her partner and tending to her vegie patch.

Mickey passed away from a stroke on 3 June 2003, at 10 years of age.

Cat, *cat*, and *Cat*

Patricia Sykes

🐾 **Patricia Sykes** *is an award-winning Australian poet. Her first collection was* Wire Dancing *(Spinifex Press, 1999). She is completing a second with the assistance of an Australia Council Grant.*

1 Cat

she was never a howl in the night
a ginger roiling among wind
and owl, her sleek strategy
was silence, but every Sekhmet
is loathed by ailurophobes
as in Napoleon & Hitler
& Alexander-the-Great—
among the glinting predators
emperors most fear what is
beyond them to defeat   her
stealth, whose secret hours
I crept among as if I could
become a Weir Tiger at will
a cat of the spirit, silk
of the wild eye, and still, and
even so, my eight-year-old
heart fell into small talk,
naming her, *Ginny,* epithet
for a beseeched pet, Ginny
of the order of resistance
her appetite so fed by the kill
it had no greed for the hand's
affections, this reach that tracks
her yet among cat language's
hundred mysterious sounds
writing entrapment symbolisms
such as *my lioness of hunger*
and *the engine of my hunt*

2 *cat*

our share-house beast, a swift
black italic, around legs, through
windows, whenever eyes were too
much upon her or hands encroached
as if witch history had squeezed
her bones too hard, and sometimes
dark fire leaping from her pelt
as if an old pyre still burned there
yet on Canasta Fridays she sat
among us like an Alice cat
the Cheshire look, maddening
and aloof as we won or lost
and even when we tossed
the idiot cards into flight
she refused to rise to the bird
though once at a coming-of-age
she allowed herself to be held
jowl-to-cheek for a camera's
blackmagic, sublimely meek
until the floor again sped
beneath her and she was gone
the night a hissing velvet
a tuft of fur in my fingers
the end of a gaming run
a spill of trumps, a dud hand

3 *Cat*

a male Siamese, creamy, elegant
epitome of sub-tropic languor
and condition of no protection
against the reigning tom's
humping fetish the owner's
fix though was laughter and
oblivion in esoteric things
but the woman who repeatedly
played witness took notes
as if the raids proved macho
neurosis' need to be on top
in the language of dominant
sex but wasn't the tom merely
enacting top-cat abberrations?
and the woman was merely
between roads, a temporary
pair of arms for cat stress, so
how did she omit to remember
that the country of shelter
is no permanence?   though
of course there's no moral in it
only the way the woman had
of emptying herself into
the beck and call of place
so that in the hinterland
where her arms briefly were
a Siamese *slinks under the sun's*
hot light bulb, attempts continuously
to evade the violence of surprise
and the laws of belonging
wear a question mark for a tail

The Master of the House

Di Brown

When Kung reached maturity he went about his black-and-white business with such style that he could easily have been the butler. This would have raised class issues in our feminist household and besides, this was utterly beneath his dignity. Living in a lesbian household, Kung was dubbed The Man of the House and his nickname stuck. What is it about the alchemy of black-and-white cats that make them so special? Just ask any woman who has ever lived with one or more. Kung's sexuality was pretty much a non-issue after the snip but his sensuality was something else, exuding from every pore/paw. As a kitten his agility and strength were astounding. He would run at walls or any other physical barrier and jump at them, pushing off with his back legs. To run my hands over his strong back and body and feel him respond was absolute pleasure. His physical strength and animal power were indeed desirable. Tucked away under his top coat was a glossy layer of deep red henna fur. When napping, Kung had a distinct way of resting the side of his head on his outstretched left front leg. He would follow me around the house or the garden, talking all the way. How I miss the familiar sound of his feline paws on the stairs, his deep rumbling purr and yes, even his daily demands.

On the day I made the decision about Kung, a big old river red that would have outlived us all was finally cut down. This tree was the centre of a local community debate and its days too were numbered, not because it posed a real threat but because it was perceived as a threat. The tree leaned out and over an historic old bridge near Ferguson's Paddock that carries much of the vehicle and pedestrian traffic near the town of Hurstbridge where we live. After months of deliberation, the shire council moved quickly and quietly and only a few mid-morning walkers witnessed the event. Those who do not value the green wedge shire will drive over the bridge, totally unaware that the tree ever existed. For those of us who do and outlive the river red, we cannot forget.

The decision to euthanase Kung was made for very different reasons and yet to my mind, these two events are very much connected. Kung had been diagnosed with diabetes but he was insulin resistant. The pig insulin wasn't working and blood tests finally revealed acromegaly, a rare disease characterised by the over-growth of connective tissue, membranous bone and viscera due to abnormal and excessive secretion of growth hormone. Although Kung was fourteen years of age and in the prime of his life, his body was still trying to grow. The disease inhibited the transport of glucose into his cells, causing an exhaustion of pancreatic ß-cells and this resulted in insulin-resistant diabetes mellitus.

The results of an Australian study on another cat with acromegaly, conducted at the University of Melbourne Veterinary Hospital at Werribee have been published. This cat, a black-and-white short-haired domestic male, was the same age as Kung. One year after initial presentation and management of his insulin-resistant diabetes he had been euthanased. Kung managed to live a little longer. A pituitary mass was growing at the base of his brain, putting him at risk of congenital heart disease, or lung or renal failure due to thickening tissue. His progressive neurological symptoms were caused by the expansion of the mass. His body shape changed and continued to change but he escaped the terrible distortions characteristic of many acromegaly cats, featuring a broadened face and elongated mandible.

Kung's breathing had become increasingly laboured. In shock and out of twice daily habit, I gave Kung his final insulin shot and an hour later the vet administered a lethal dose of anaesthetic. My beautiful black-and-white boy died peacefully in my arms. A friend in Hobart who had lived for many years with her own black-and-white, sent me Gwen Harwood's poem Feline Requiem. One line in the poem says it all and partly explains the connection with the tree. 'We outlive so many loves.'

The last five years of Kung's life were spent in the company of Zoyra, my partner's red and white Siberian husky. Dealing with Zoyra's boisterous puppy energy was over the top for Kung although as Zoyra matured, and Kung felt less threatened, they had their moments together. I've enjoyed an enduring passion for black-and-white cats, and have lived with and cared for several. When Kung was first diagnosed with diabetes and the vet detailed his daily care, I burst into tears. My partner, Kiersten, was previously diagnosed with acute lymphoblastic leukemia, had fought hard, survived the treatment and to this day remains in remission. The thought of taking on the role of primary carer all over again just felt overwhelming. The reward, of course, was to have Kung with us for another year, knowing as we do that Life is a precious gift.

Di Brown would like to be reborn in her next life as a much loved black-and-white cat. In this life she has been instructed and rewarded by the many animals she has befriended. 🐾

Paean for Psyche

Elizabeth Dias

ties of a tiger
beautiful umbilical
angel coiled in sleep

beautiful ties
my umbilical angel
coiled in tiger-sleep

angel beautiful
ties coiled umbilical
sleep my tiger sleep

Elizabeth Dias *is a Melbourne designer and illustrator who spent several halcyon childhood years in country West Australia in a house surrounded by cats (a dozen, at one count). Her love for cats is boundless, and she feels especially blessed when they cross dark, late-night streets to greet her—a stranger—to receive long, drawn-out pats.* 🐾

Says Woman to Cat

Koa Whittingham

Majestic, noble, regal
You can even fall off a chair,
With dignity

Confident, grand, self-assured
You command the attention of the room,
And expect affection

Certain, secure, assertive
We call but you take a message,
And get back to us

We've been through some bad times
Burning times
Dark times
Ignorant times
Terrible times
We've been hated together

And I admire you,
Says Woman to Cat,
I admire you,
My dear little friend
We've been burnt, oppressed and cursed,
But you've never forgotten, we were worshipped first.

Koa Whittingham *is a twenty-two-year-old woman from Brisbane. She has a Bachelor of Arts degree in philosophy and a Bachelor of Science degree in psychology from the University of Queensland and is continuing studies in psychology, with the aim of being a clinical psychologist. She has always loved writing stories and poetry and is currently working on a novel.*

Olivia — Kim Mann

daily she stalks
the mortal sins of pride plus two

stones the world with her stare
the time and dignity of admiration

makes her silver silent speaking
at the window

imagines birds
watches for the movement of faint wind

in the Norfolk Island pines
she is waiting

carefully she smooths down her hair each morning
in the dusty reflection

then sits in the sun, dreams
looks over at you

she's come to you with this strange attraction
your hands and her head

she wants your touch, now
will lay her body under your hand

and her love might leave a speckling of dried
blood; red freckles on your pale skin

she will turn you over in artifice
and teach you a life not hers

knows well
the Art of psychology in reverse

on occasion I mistake
silence for listening and try to speak

you ignore me, my words a century in your ears
while you sleep, walk, eat

she moves with all the freedom
of a spirit through this world
and she's efficient my lady, can demonstrate
vaguely annoyed with a twitch of the face

deals with conceit and love
daily

she'll pine and she'll moan
when she wants you badly, to play

other times, give such a small signal
that this is beginning again

just by the eyes
when her low breath comes and I know

and she will take you in delight and a luxury of limbs
playing joy like an instrument

but then there's the moment when
you know it's enough

because she'll pull her chin in
and tilt her head a little away

to indicate the greatest disdain
9 lives of emotions in one day

I do not inhabit her world
now or ever

but know I will turn in my sleep
one night and meet her black lips

look into the envy of those green eyes
I adore you, you suffocate me

—your hands, baby leather
the warm smell of your sleep

as I nuzzle my nose and face into
your soft belly and look up

your eyes
my old lover

 Kim Mann *grew up in Alice Springs and*
has lived in England and America. With
over forty poems published in journals,
books and newspapers, she has attended
events and festivals around Australia. She
has written and published short stories, a
play and a libretto for a concert with the
ASO. Kim holds an MA and is now writing
her first novel.

Zen and the Art of Human Resource Management...

Ruth Blaikie

The following is a copy of a letter I inadvertently stumbled upon that my cat, Zen, had sent to my friend, who used to share a house with us. Or should I say, Zen allowed us to share his house with him.

dear aunty sandy

You would not believe what has happened to me this week. You know I am the most handsome cat in the neighbourhood ('my own little All Black,' Mummy says) with the most stylish purple collar with sparkly gold studs (appropriate I feel as, just quietly, I am a bit of a stud myself). So I was quite shocked to hear one ignorant moggy call me Liberace. Sorted him out pretty quickly! Got a bit tired after that for a few days, although it didn't put me off my nosh, but Mummy wondered why my face was swelling up, followed by icky marks left on the corner of her duvet where I sleep. And then I ended up with a bald patch as the gruesome area healed. Had to stay inside for a few days as I didn't want my handsome reputation to be compromised in the street.

Of course, there are repercussions to staying inside for too long (although I did pop outside briefly as necessary). But while inside, getting bored and watching the rain, I decided to do a spot of interior decorating. As you know, my beloved Mummy, bless her, has no decorative style, so I was somewhat astonished, after spending a considerable amount of time spazzing about rearranging the rug in the lounge and the contents on the coffee table, aerating the couch and curtains with my personal signature claws, to find on Mummy's return from work, that my expertise was not much appreciated. Had to do some fast smooching, grovelling,

being sweet and quite frankly, sickly (don't tell anyone) if there was to be any hope at all of getting fed that night. But as you know, the woman is putty in my paws.

Alas the story doesn't end there. As the man of the house—even though I had my brains removed while barely out of my kitten attire—it is beholden to me to be the hunter-gatherer. After all, the dear old girl hasn't managed to bag a husband yet, so someone has to step up to the mark! So, dutifully, off I trot to do my bit for queen and country. This cave-cat thing takes some time and skill so when I finally returned, Mummy had retired to bed. Not being the shy type, I launched myself boldly through the cat flap with my latest catch grasped firmly between my fearful jaws. One has the responsibility to have a bit of fun while doing one's chivalrous duty, so I proceeded to torment my victim for as long as possible. As we all know, the best laid plans of cats and men rarely go smoothly and, rather miffed at being woken up at some ungodly hour, Mother (note the loss of soft endearment) leaped out of bed and switched the light on. Well… all hell broke loose.

What I hadn't realised was that, while it was kind of okay to bring in the odd wee mouse or skink or cricket, apparently rats are out of the question. In the turmoil of some hasty redecorating on my part once again, purely to distract her from catching me and biffing me outside, the rat ran under her bed. Mummy's not noted for her Mary Poppins tidiness, so the rat found a few cosy hidey corners in which to claim sanctuary. I do admire the woman though. Realising the battle was temporarily over, my lovely Mummy shrugged her shoulders, switched off the light and went back to bed—at least I think that's what she did. I had, meanwhile,

beaten a hasty retreat to the safety of the wide-open spaces outside.

Sadly Ratty did not fare so well. The next day she caught it as it scuttled behind the door, chucked it in a bucket and hastily covered it with a towel as it was doing a very good impression of an Olympic high jumper. Being a bit of a softy when it comes to small furry creatures (lucky for me), Mummy was all for putting it back into the wild, but her brother had other ideas and duly bashed Ratty all over and then chucked it!

Anyway Aunty Sandy, it's time for some cuddles, so I'd better go and grease around Mummy with a bit of purring thrown in just to fool her. (The fact that it's rapidly approaching dinnertime is neither here nor there.)

Before you impulsively respond, let me remind you of that old adage: *'Dogs have masters; cats have staff.'* Like gravity, it just is.

Love and scratches

Ruth Blaikie is a single woman in her extreme thirties from Auckland, New Zealand. There was always a cat at home when she was growing up, and she has often wondered what really goes on in their tiny little minds.

Aubade

Aileen Kelly

Seven ay em two codeine
and snarl
at the cat who strokes
her purring furry flank
and lank muffled hip
along my ankle. Drink
deep water to tide out the tablets
and set the bladder-clock
then curl back to bed with a tickle
of loose fur on the footskin.
If she's moulting it
might be Spring but
awake on schedule
at eleven it's still
Autumn and overcast
and all the available kisses
smell of sardine.

Aileen Kelly *is a poet and adult educator, who grew up (with her mother's cat) in England, and now lives in Melbourne, where for many years Sandy The Cat was the only other female in her household.*

Koci Mama (Cat's Mother)

Rose Kizinska

'Shut up Rose,' yelled Miss Partiasio, my grade six teacher at a catholic primary school. 'You are just so *catty*.'

'What does that mean Miss?' (thinking that I needed to know, before I came back at her with another line).

'It means you're a *bitch*.'

'So…let's see…does that make me a cat or a dog then?'

Now I have chosen to belong to the pussycat, the Kizia, just like my maternal grandmother did before she was married and became necessary, vital, indispensable: a Konieczny. Once, I was a seed on a twig on the branch of a sycamore (Jawor) tree: spinning endlessly, rotating like manic little helicopter blades, shedding out of control, until I found that Kizia fits better on my skin.

My mother has cat's eyes. It's her view of the world. Green, prismatic and perceptive but, in other ways, too green. My mum's favourite, Casper, went into the compost heap one day and placed a kitten from there in each of our laps, one by one. We had returned home after over a year of running away from our father.

In my mother's house, three months later, Gizmo, who had lived through her kittenhood with my sisters and I in a dingy flat, gave birth to five kittens on top of the washing machine. She abandoned all of them and no amount of milk in eyedroppers could save them. It wasn't too long after that I left home again.

During my final stay with my mother, several years later, Ruby, as a gutter-saved, flea-ridden, swollen-gutted kitten, came with me. On the first night, I tucked her under the covers. Mum unceremoniously woke me that morning, describing how she'd spent the last hour picking worms out of Ruby. I don't think I have ever flown out of bed as fast, neither before nor since then. I guess after five children, nothing shocks her anymore.

At Movie World in Queensland, my mother insisted on photographing me with Cat Woman: slinky rubber suit, whip and all. In hawker centers across Singapore, I fed scraps to the sleek, tailless street cats, under the table. In Hong Kong, I floated through the endless array of mouthless Hello Kittys and made sure I brought home enough of them for my collection. In Dallas the snow white CT (recently RIP L) kept me warm, during my first ever snow and sleet-stained winter and Chester (the massive table-top, on squat legs) threatened to crush me with a single bound, while I waited everyday for my new love, Silverkat, to come home to me from school. But it was Ruby who for ten years or so made every, almost yearly, move with me. Never complaining, always adapting, so long as I never left her for too long.

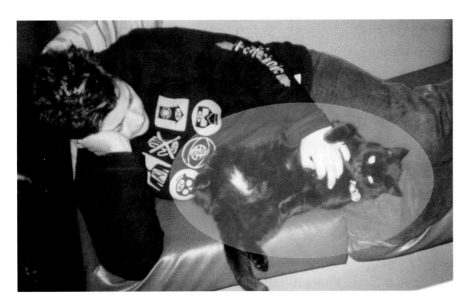

Ruby Queen of the Bed once said, as she walked across the arm of a past lover, who now has her, 'So, this is whom you've left me for, on all those cold lonely winter nights, when I've had to help myself to the crunchies in the cupboard.' That night, I give her warm KFC for dinner and her favourite can of fruit salad for dessert.

When I was a toddler, two smooth snooty black cats lived at my grandmother's house. I yearned for them to like me more because, before I started school, I lived there too. I don't remember this. I only know it to be so because my mother let the cat out of the bag, so to speak, only two years ago. I only remember the lullaby, the one that begins, 'ahhh, ahhh… kotki dwa…' (two kittens), which used to soothe me to sleep.

Ruby is fiercely independent, belonging to no one but me. Driving down the road with another girl in the same town: a black cat wearing a red collar lying rigid on the nature strip, on the same road where I had left her one year ago. I stand beside her, heart aching, tears pouring. 'It's Ruby, it's Ruby. I know it's my girl.' Visions drench me, of my Ruby's face poking out of my karate sports bag, on the tram, on the way to the vet, a few times, more than a few years ago. I have to know if it's my Ruby. It has been a year now. Could I be mistaken?

I can't step foot in that front yard again to check; the land that was mine, with the big old oak tree, the house isn't mine anymore. It's been a year. I open the gate and see a cat more Rubyesque than the one on the nature strip, with that puffy-cheeked face and those accusing jade eyes. I telepathically communicate to her that I have a home again. She can come with me.

I call her, 'Ruby, Ruby', and she sits still and stares. I walk towards her, pick her up and hold her tight. If I put her down and call her, if she comes, she is mine, always has been mine and I'll take her away, I will. 'Ruby, Ruby…Kizia, Kizi, Kiz, Kiz…' She sits and stares, content under the oak tree and unforgiving that I had left her.

As the jasmine breathes its scent all night, my Silverkat lies beside me, snuggles in and purrs: out of the cyberworld and into the real. From somewhere close to Sycamore Illinois she came, to be right by her only Kizia: Me.

Rose Kizinska is currently living her sixth life outta' nine. Maybe in this one, she will finally finish her MA novel and get a 'real job'. For right now, she is content to lie about the house with her Silverkat, tell stories and dream. 🐾

What's in a Name?

Coralie McLean

In recent years, I have been blessed with two adorable cats who chose to share their lives with me. As is the way with cats, they took over my territory and made it their own.

The first was a rather strange-looking, but totally bewitching, grey Burmese. She turned up at my home and starting hanging around. She was lean and scrawny and, not knowing much about cats, I thought she must be a stray, or even a feral cat. For the first few days, we studiously ignored each other, but at the first sign of invitation, she sidled up to me and was rewarded with a bowl of milk. The poor thing, she was starving (or so I thought), so how could I do otherwise? Before I knew it, she had established a routine and I had a cupboard stocked with various delicacies suitable for restoring a languishing cat to robust health and taming the savage beast.

It looked like she had decided to abandon her feral ways and was planning to stay awhile. If so, she had to have a name. I decided on Wildcat, after Mary Daly's talented cat made famous in the pages of her book *Outercourse—The Be-Dazzling Voyage*. Quickly (my) Wildcat became known among my family and friends as the 'little scrap' who had my heart in thrall. They were bemused by the name Wildcat—she was small, somewhat straggly, a little battered and the worse for wear and, on first acquaintance, didn't seem to suit the name. However I had already glimpsed the strong spirit, the brave soul and the loving heart and, now that she was mine, Wildcat it was to be.

But was she 'mine'? She acted as if she was but, one day, just a few weeks after her insinuation into my space, the neighbour from next-door-but-one came calling. 'Hello, I live two doors down and I just wanted to see if my old cat is in your garden. She's been away from home for a while and I thought she may be here. Ah, there she is. Hello, Cindy Sue, are you coming home with me?'

What?! Her cat! Not a feral cat or even a stray? A cosseted, cared-for, domestic specimen whose home was just down the road! And her name was *Cindy Sue?* Not at all the sort of name I associated with this little amazon.

After the neighbour departed, the cat and I looked at each other. It had only been a few weeks, but my heart was hurting as I said to the little cat who stayed sitting there blinking at me, 'Go home! You're not *my* cat!' and turned and walked away.

But, as is also the way with cats, she had her own thoughts and ideas about this and she obviously concluded that a compromise could be found. She decided she could cope with two names so, even though I no longer fed her (she hopped the fence and returned to her home for dinner each night), Wildcat spent much time with me, gradually encroaching on more and more of my space until things I initially regarded as unthinkable (not on my bed!) were eventually accepted by me as rightfully hers. And, of course, *I* was hers.

She was a loving presence in my life for two-and-a-half years and when the time came for her to die, she died at my home, with me, and I thought my heart would break.

In the months following Wildcat's death, I considered the option of sharing my home with another cat, but somehow it all seemed too much when I thought of having sole responsibility (rather than the convenient 'shared custody' that I had enjoyed with Wildcat) and having to arrange for feeding and caring for those frequent periods when my work involved travel away. However, things have a way of happening...

In October 2000, a friend and I set off on the 'great feminist adventure'. That year saw the fulfillment of a unique dream of a group of Canadian women to create a world wide event—the World March of Women 2000. A virtual march, it was based on the concept of rallies and marches occurring in countries across the world in the six-month period from March to October. The theme was the elimination of poverty and violence against women and the culminating event was a huge rally in New York.

We made it to that amazing event in New York and joined with tens of thousands of women from countries across the world in a spectacular show of women's strength and solidarity. It was a wonderful experience, enriched by the opportunity we took to travel to the US via Italy. Our arrival in Italy coincided with the World March events there and we took to the streets of Rome with several thousand wonderful, vibrant women whose enthusiasm was undaunted by the teeming rain that fell.

Returning home in late October, inspired, energised and awash with vivid memories, the last thing I expected was to find that, in my absence, a cat had taken up residence. A creature of beauty—a large, smoke-grey Persian—she had clearly been loved and cherished, but was now obviously in trouble. She was hungry but was finding it difficult to eat. Her fur was knotted and her eyes were pleading.

I went through the process of seeking her owner—but no one came forward. I then considered how to find a good home for her, but this cat seemed to have other ideas and was rapidly settling in at my place. Hour by hour, she was also settling into my heart. In no time, I had capitulated—it looked like my next cat had arrived and I would just have to cope.

The first step was a visit to the vet and that was illuminating. I found out four things:

1. she was about eight years old;

2. she appeared to have been on her own and 'doing it tough' for a few months, at least;

3. she was basically healthy, but had a widespread infection in her gums which would necessitate an urgent operation to remove a number of teeth; and

4. she was a he!

Oh well, this last revelation called for a bit of mental adjustment, as well as a jettisoning of all the strong feminist names I had been toying with.

My soul was still full of Italy, so an Italian name it had to be for this fine fellow—a name redolent of the sights and sounds of that intoxicating country. My new *gatto* became Luca.

Wildcat had been agile, engaging, clever and curious. Luca is slow and plodding, dignified and self-contained. He needs to do very little to win admiration and affection and so that is what he does—very little. However, he is good-natured and patient and he allows me to share his space with equanimity.

As cats go, the Wondrous Wildcat and Luca the Lovely are opposites, but they have enthralled me in equal measure. Each padded softly into my life and decided to stay awhile. Each has intrigued and entranced me and taught me much. Both have been gifts from the goddess.

Coralie McLean has a background in social work and is a committed feminist activist. She has had a long-time involvement in women's services in Townsville and was one of the organisers of the very successful Townsville International Women's Conference in July 2002. She has always been a dog lover but, with the arrival of Wildcat, found she is just as susceptible to the fathomless charms of cats.

familiar

rebecca anderson

there are cat people and there are dog people. cat people rest with the quiet assurance that cats are indeed the supreme beings; smarter than dolphins even. fey is a good word: feral, cunning, stunning, adorable. capable of inciting adoration left, right, above, below, within.

my cat is master of the universe. prince of shadow. shadow cat. lord of all creation. cats really do have secret names i think and, despite his neutering easily eight years ago, he retains a distinctly masculine air. or perhaps i simply mistake imperiousness as a masculine trait?

because of him i believe in telepathy—for i am woken by the piercing gaze that transmits the desire for either breakfast or a change of litter. the vocal requests (for yes, he does speak) begin as soon as my feet touch the morning floor or as the threshold to the kitchen is crossed.

because of him i believe in reincarnation, soul mates and love at first sight. underneath everything is the energy of life, of nature. a completeness that can only compare with twilight of certain rainforests lit by the yellow moon. because of him i know that we never really choose cats. they choose us.

cats have a way of owning you completely. there is the theory that cats are aloof. paul isn't—he may be the exception that proves the rule. generous and liberal with his affections, he can work a room with more sincerity and charisma than the most compelling politician imaginable, with a never failing instinct, drawn to the person he hasn't yet charmed to full capacity. i don't exaggerate. some say their cat is the best cat in the world. maybe paul isn't the best, but let me tell you he is in the top ten.

when i look into his eyes i never fail to be astounded by the being i encounter. there is a mind there. quite human, but not. i secretly suspect that out of the two of us he is the higher intelligence. he certainly has me well trained.

a grey ball of purring, curling, head tucked under a paw. wrapped neatly in a tail. a tailor-made lap warmer or sitting sphinx like, ears and paws four square, with eyes yellow-green and black that plug me straight to the heart of the universe.

reb is an actor-director-performance artist-quietly freaking out that she is about to turn thirty without the benefit of a mortgage. paul, her cat still loves her though.

Ned
Nancy Winters

I'm creating poetry.

So is my cat, Ned.

I'm reaching deep in my soul.

He's cleaning his head.

Nancy Winters *lives in London.*
She is a novelist, poet, travel writer and
Woman of a Certain Age whom strays
and other people's cats have helped
along the way to the life of her dreams.
She has never had a kitten.

Permissions

Suniti Namjoshi, p173: 'Deaf Eurydice' was previously published in *Kavya Bharati*, No.12, 2000, American College, Madurai, India, and on the Internet Residency in Poetry for The Commonwealth Institute web site London, (10 February–8 May 1999.)

Susan Wiseheart, p36: A different version of this piece was previously published in *Maize: A Country Lesbian Magazine*, Summer 2002.

Photographs

pix Naomi McKercher; px Anne Quain; p2 Blaise Van Hek; p6 Annabel Fagan; p7 Beverley Hall; p8, 9 Lorraine Williams; p17 Pieter Kant; p20 (left) Bronwyn Whitlocke; p22, 23 Cathie Dunsford; p25 Daniel Torpy; p26, 29 Michael Goldsmith; p30 Anne Quain; p32, 34, 35 Deb Ball; p36 Susan Wiseheart; p37 Carole Wiseheart Jensen; p40, 43 Cathy Larsen; p45 Susan Hawthorne; p47 Robyn Adams; p49 Ashley Wong Hoy; p60 Sabina Rees; p62 Jan Weate; p63 Sal Hampson, p65 (left) M.McIntyre, (right) Jan Weate; p66 Anne Quain; p68, 71 Robyn Adams; p73 Jan Thorburn; p77 Kathryn Cott; p78 Bronwyn Whitlocke; p79 Michael Fletcher; p81, 82 (left) Margaret Young, (right) Morag Young; p84, 85 Janine Le Couteur; p88 Kate Marquard; p91 Coral Hull; p96 Joyce Redding; p99, 101 Sharman Horwood; p106 Jill Wilson; p113 Tricia Dasic; p122, 125 Conchita Fonseca; p129 Dora Levakis; p130 Michael Quain; p131,132 Tanya Grassi; p133 Jamie Fawcett; p135 Steffen Pedersen; p136 Keith Ottaway; p142,143 Patricia Best; p145 Lavender; p148 Lynette Benjamin; p149 Andrew Polotnianka; p153 Linda Morra; p155 June Clay; p156,157 Chris Brown; p158 Anne Quain; p160 (left) Bridget Musters, (right) Ann Musters; p171 G. Ross; p173 Gillian Hanscombe; p178, 179 C.K. Fearn; p180 William Thompson; p183 Prosser Stirling; p185 Lesley Fowler & S.Edgar; p186 Terry Quinn/ Joan Marchant Cardew; p188,189 Ira Wood; p190,193 Anthony & Melony Stott; p197 Kiersten Coulter; p201 Cathy Whittingham; p205 (top) Ruth Blaikie, (bottom) Ken Blaikie; p213 Coralie McLean; p215 Carole Moschetti; p216 Monica Curtin; p217 (top) Nancy Winters, (bottom) J. Barry O'Rourke

All other photographs are from the personal collections of individuals named in the text. The publisher acknowledges kind permission to reproduce these photographs.

Other books by Jan Fook

Transforming Social Work Practice
Breakthroughs in Practice
Radical Casework
Professional Expertise (co-author)
Critical Social Work in Changing Contexts (forthcoming)
The Reflective Researcher (editor)
Transforming Social Work Practice (co-editor)
Practice and Research in Social Work (co-editor)
Breakthroughs in Practice (co-editor)

Other books by Susan Hawthorne

The Falling Woman
Wild Politics: Feminism, Globalisation and Bio/diversity
September11, 2001: Feminist Perspectives (co-editor)
Bird and other writings on epilepsy
Car Maintenance, Explosives and Love and other lesbian writings (co-editor)
The Spinifex Quiz Book
The Language in My Tongue
The Exploding Frangipani: Lesbian Writing from Australia and New Zealand (co-editor)
Moments of Desire: Sex and Sensuality by Australian Feminist Writers (co-editor)
Difference: Writings by Women

Other books by Renate Klein

Infertility: Women Speak Out about their Experiences of Reproductive Medicine
The Exploitation of a Desire
The Ultimate Colonisation: Reproductive and Genetic Engineering
RU 486: Misconceptions, Myths and Morals (co-author)
Theories of Women's Studies (co-editor)
Test-Tube Women (co-editor)
Radical Voices (co-editor)
Radically Speaking: Feminism Reclaimed (co-editor)

Joint books

A Girl's Best Friend: The Meaning of Dogs in Women's Lives (Jan Fook and Renate Klein)
CyberFeminism: Connectivity, Critique and Creativity (Susan Hawthorne and Renate Klein)
Australia for Women: Travel and Culture (Susan Hawthorne and Renate Klein)
Angels of Power and other reproductive creations (Susan Hawthorne and Renate Klein)

A GIRL'S BEST FRIEND: THE MEANING OF DOGS IN WOMEN'S LIVES

Jan Fook and Renate Klein (eds)

ISBN 1-876756-10-1

Over eighty stories, poems and autobiography, from women and girls about their relationships with dogs. Funny, sad, memorable; readers will laugh and cry as they read this beautifully illustrated book about their best friend.

'Finally, a dog book to recommend unequivocally'
– Debra Adelaide, *Sydney Morning Herald*

'... it is quite possible you won't be able to put this book down'
– Shaunagh O'Connor, *Herald Sun*

'If you are a dog owner, you cannot help but bask in the supreme feeling of justice that these wonderful creatures have finally received the recognition they deserve.'
– *Conscious Living, Summer*

If you would like to know more about Spinifex Press, write for a free catalogue or visit our Web site.

Spinifex Press
PO Box 212, North Melbourne
Victoria 3051, Australia
www.spinifexpress.com.au